ADAM, THE LAST MAN

THE WHISPER

An Allegorical Novel

CANDYCE L. NICHOLS

By Candyce L. Nichols

Editing by Deirdre Lockhart at Brilliant Cut Editing. Cover art by Adam Nichols. Photo by Joshua Earle on Unsplash.

CONTENTS

WHAT IF GOD...?

If we take a look at mankind, one obvious fact about us is that we are complainers. The biggest complaint of mankind is that we don't think that God is doing His part. If He is such a good God, we ask, then why does He let sin keep going? And why can't He just make it all stop? "If I were God, I would..." people protest. "I would do this, or I would do that!" This usually happens when there is no relationship with God Almighty and biblical education is nil. This book is investigating one of those situations of "What if God handled it this way?"

CHAPTER 1

IN THE BEGINNING, IT HAPPENED!

"I have loved you," says the Lord.

"Yet you say, 'In what way have You loved us?' " Malachi 1:2 (NKJ)

Before we begin this story, you must think about what's going on right now. People are doing so many different things. For example, they are eating, driving, sleeping, working, dancing. Or they could be hitting, cursing, torturing, doing drugs, hurting children, stealing, killing, and so on. Take a breath! I tried to think of everything humans are doing right now, and I had to give up. It's too much. There are those who are being operated on, flying planes, and yes, praying. And at a moment in time like now, "it" happened.

It happened in just a fragment of a moment all around the world, at the same time, when *God spoke.*

He spoke in a way that allowed one to pass right into their next thought with ease. Later in time, one would be able to recall and say, "Yes. I remember I did have that thought." It didn't shake the earth, nor did people tremble or scream out, "God has spoken to me!" But it was delivered and delivered discreetly, like the moment when the Christ child breathed His first breath. So, what was it God said? "There will be no more children."

At first, 90 percent of the human population didn't even notice. They went right on doing whatever they were doing. However, the next day, when some Christians awoke, they began to share in small ways, like when two sisters or close friends would converse about a dream they may have had. Some reacted with a what-if? Others checked their Bibles, and a few pondered.

As you could guess, the first to observe an odd crack in man's usual clock were the doctors. No new patients were passing through their doors after a certain amount of time. Then, as the strange news passed from doctor to doctor, there came a pause and then a great gasp. Then the real shuddering started, and the questions came. "What could be causing this? Could it have been a sunburst resulting in some sort of strange radiation?" A reasonable theory, except there had been none. "Could there have been some poison released by a terrorist?" They were heartless, but they didn't process technology capable of such magnitude. Even everything doctors had stored from men and women, the cells refused to bring forth life.

So, when the world broadcast reporters received this frightening affirmation, they delivered it with shaking hands. And those who had aborted their children out of convenience wept.

CHAPTER 2

GOD'S CHOSEN

Let me now tell you about this one couple God the Father handpicked. Marlene and Jon Stands were chosen by God to raise the last child ever to be born. One could say they were blessed and cursed because of this predestined package, but God knew what He was doing. He picked this family with their strong God-fearing values to fulfill His assignment. God would add one more to this large family of six children—three boys and three girls—to be the beginning of the end.

At first, Marlene had no signs or symptoms that she was with another child. But, when she was about five months along, she felt a life. Certainly, one would think a mother of six would be experienced in the signs of pregnancy. But God had concealed her seventh from her because, when the worldwide news reports confirmed that there were no more pregnancies, people began to steal babies or make monetary offers for the unborn ones.

Evil had not taken time off, though people knew way down deep that God was who spoke. God also knew there would be those who would still refuse to look to Him. Because of this age-old independence, each mother was chained to fear while trying to protect her children, born or unborn.

In the five months since God spoke, a tsunami of panic flooded each country. The knees of mankind buckled as he grasped the news, along with an unstoppable crumbling financial world. Man was having to accept it as a well-lit fuse leading to his final destruction. So the existence of all man had built and loved was now an avalanching around him.

Consider how you would be thinking. Questions like, "What do you want to be when you grow up?" would take on a new meaning. You would be thinking about the moment when there would no longer be any electricity. *How will we take care of ourselves when we get old?* As the words of God became fact, people succumbed to fear, and in this fear, they showed their inner hearts, good or evil.

CHAPTER 3

CONGRATULATIONS! IT'S THE LAST BOY!

These chosen Christian parents, Jon and Marlene Stands, ran their farm home with a *Little House on the Prairie* atmosphere. Marlene homeschooled all of her children, ages six through seventeen, not only giving them education but also a good set of values and lots of love.

But, now, they were forced to look at their children's questionable future. Jon and Marlene began the task of recalculating all of it. The children were no longer encouraged to have college goals. Shakespeare was not important. These children *needed* to know how to live in a shrinking world. They contemplated the world their last child would inherit with his adulthood. By then, this world would be not only sad and scary but also baffling.

Even though Marlene was way overdue, she had been spending most of the morning working with her pride and joy—her garden—with several of her younger children. Having to take another break, she eased her very pregnant body down onto her wooden garden bench. *Okay, little Adam, I shall sit and rest again.* Leaning back, she closed her eyes and listened to her younger children call out. "Outcha go, Pete!" and "No more of you, Mary Sue!"

They were stone naming—a game she invented for the children. Whenever they found an unwanted rock nestled in the garden, they named it and cast it out.

With her eyes still closed, she savored the familiar sound of Jon and his horse near the barn. Every day for the last four weeks, he found some reason to leave whatever he was working on to come back to check up on her, and she loved it.

She gazed down at her stomach. It rolled from one lump and one peaked bump to another as if this child were stretching and arching its back. Then it came… an intense twinge!

Rounding the barn on the dirt path, Jon stopped as he studied her, probably wondering what she was thinking so intently with her head tilted like that.

"Marlene!" His shout startled her. "I have seen that look on your face maybe six other times. Am I right?"

A smile scrunching face, she nodded. "Maybe. Give me some time to be sure."

"Hon." Jon laughed. "You've got to be kidding. You have had six babies already, and you're two weeks overdue. Do you really think you need more time?" Shaking his head in obvious unbelief, he offered her a hand up. "Or maybe you would like to have this child in the garden?"

"Well, his name will be Adam, so what better place?" She winked.

While leaning forward, she cradled her stomach with one hand and reached for his with the other. Then she cramped again "Oh boy, let's go. I do not want to have my baby in a garden!"

"Okay, that's it. We are done."

Dr. Karen Woods had just finished stitching up a woman's stomach from a hysterectomy when a nurse burst through the operating room door, holding a mask to her face. Leaning in to the doctor's ear, she whispered, "Marlene's on her way!"

Karen turned to the nurse and asked, "Is everything okay?" while trying to read what little she could see of her eyes.

"As far as I know. But it is her seventh, and she is way too late."

Karen accepted that this was to be not only her last delivery but possibly also the whole world's. The news had been eerily quiet for the past seven days with not one report of another birth.

She removed her gloves and mask, sterilized her hands, and exited the room, leaving Mrs. Kirkwood in capable hands, post-surgery. Quick steps carried her away from the OR toward, not the maternity ward. And with each step, her heart beat faster than usual. What was wrong with her? How many babies had she brought into the world? She shouldn't be trembling.

Three weeks ago, she'd begged Marlene to move into the hospital—for their safety, but Marlene wouldn't have it. So, every two days since, Karen showed up at the farm, concluding Marlene was safer out of sight.

Having planned for this arrival, Karen had instructed Marlene to enter through a door used only for those deceased. She also handpicked discreet nursing staff, who took it upon themselves to keep this child and mother hidden from the public eye.

When all was in order, and by God's own hand, Adam Malachi Stands took his first beautiful breath.

Moments later, with the birthing-room chores completed in a last rite of human passage, this chosen group gathered around him and his mother in wonderment. His movements were slow, but when the child moved his head, he looked deep in their eyes with his own, connecting.

A rush of tremulous questions whispered through the room:

"Is this the last baby ever to be born?"

"I wonder what he will face."

"Why is this happing?"

And then the tears flowed.

CHAPTER 4

IT'S WHERE THEY ALL STOOD, THE STANDS

During the first five years of Adam's life, he knew nothing of this world's changing ways. He only knew when Mom baked cookies or that his siblings were his best friends. When the family went camping on their farm, he learned new skills—skills he thought were loads of fun. He mastered how to start a fire without matches and to use melted wax with packed lint when rain might hinder his efforts. None of this would be worth anything, though, without knowing who God is. In this family, the Bible was not just stories to be taught. The Bible was God's blueprint of why, how, where, and when and used daily for teaching, reproving, correcting, and training in righteousness, so the Stands would be equipped for all good works.

Both parents had chosen to ask Christ into their heart, never to leave them. They understood that, when God created this world, He desired to be with man. They understood why Christ died, why He rose, and why the Holy Spirit could dwell inside man afterward. Because of this relationship with the heavenly Father, they lived with a peace the world could never understand. Their children's morning prayer always reflected that simple relationship: "Good morning, heavenly Father. Thank You for today! Oh, and I love You!"

Were they perfect? No, they were just like you and me.

Adam's father was a wise man. He and Marlene thought nothing of asking the heavenly Father for advice on how to rear this family. The homeschool lessons, of course, had to change. They added lessons on medicine, engineering, and the study of food, which covered growing, preparation, and storage. They also studied practical life skills like carpentry, leather working, and sewing.

Many other families homeschooled in their area, and these groups joined into teams to help one another. These last groups of children needed to be trained like none before. And yet, the world debated silly things such as whether or not they'd allow children to play with baby dolls since there were no more babies.

When man took a good look at the map of his future, he saw a path he'd never seen before. People could no longer expect the passage into old age to be packaged up safe and snuggled for their care and comfort. Comfort? Things we daily take for granted, like all the blessings of electricity or doctors, would no longer be there. So many of the things man loves, but never counted as a blessing, would now disappear.

Man also found himself responsible for using wisdom like a chess piece. Calculated moves were necessary to overcome daily problems. Man's creations like nuclear energy had to be dealt with, or the unthinkable would happen.

In those calculations, people decided small towns were more apt to meet their needs than the paved cities could. As though going back in time, the old town meetings became the real hub of government. There, the people could seek out one another for ideas and help. As many of the large government systems shut down, these meetings became the only places people could unite, other than churches.

But these towns needed to be strong, or they would be easy to destroy. They put into motion systems of communication, medical stations, policing, food for the needy, and so on. With so much to handle, the smaller towns seemed a more capable area for the job. Towns also had to become independent from state and country governments because after a short time there would be none.

Christian-dominated areas were conducive to working together. Because of their love and kindness, people flocked to them and then, many times, preyed on them. This added greater burdens for those who were trying to do good, and some places collapsed under this pressure. Hungry people could so overload an area that they crippled not only the town but also one's own heart.

And the jobs man had created? Man had built up his lifestyle until he only knew how to receive a paycheck and then go off to a store and buy what he needed. Those types of people suffered. As many jobs disappeared and money to do daily shopping dwindled, they needed to become what they were not—*farmers*.

Once people realized they would have to become self-sufficient, they began studying the Amish. But that way of life was hard. What could take the Amish their whole life to learn… well, Rome wasn't built by a video game player. Christian or not, people suffered. When they could no longer rely on a paycheck or a handout received in front of some government office, they moved into the countryside, just taking land.

Begging families, violent groups of people, those who wanted to take what others had were daily problems. Man was dying off at the normal rate of 56 million a year, and in these twelve years, 672 million people around the world had died.

CHAPTER 5

JESUS WAS ALSO TWELVE!

The town meeting the Stands attended had gone well. This meeting focused on the extra older folk in town, their needs and care. Their close-knit community knew how it would go. They unanimously decided to put the extra elderly up a Dotty Colbert's. Her team of women, full of love and tenderness for the elderly, took on this task as if they'd won a lottery. Maybe because these women now had no small children or grandchildren to love on, the need to love and spoil something turned to the elderly. At the end of the meeting, all agreed to supply the food and needs of this team home, so the women could take care of their charges. If they needed someone to watch a family member while they worked or found someone in need of care, the place would always be open.

When the meeting ended, Adam's father approached him, and he paused from talking with his buddy, Noah Cahn. Adam grinned, thinking about how they were teased over their names ever since they'd become friends when Noah and his family moved in from Michigan seven years ago. Noah's family was Jewish, his dad a doctor. But this family would be leaving again soon to join a type of Kibbutz Jewish families set up to help one another.

After greeting the boys, Pa faced his son. "Adam, I'll need you to ride home with Grandpa again tonight, okay?"

"Sure, Pa." Now a healthy twelve-year-old, Adam flashed a genuine smile—something people often claimed they liked about him. Mature for his age, he was told when he spoke up his words came out like a nineteen-year-old's.

He followed his father outside. His family no longer used a car, but a horse and buggy. They'd spoken for years about this need for the change, but they kept up their old van for emergencies.

"Mom and I will be taking home the Miller family tonight." Pa was directing the family to his horse-drawn wagon. The Miller family consisted of twin girls, who were fifteen, and their mom. The Millers faithfully attended the town meetings by way of walking, but no one ever let them go home that way.

These last years, his father insisted Adam should come along to the town meetings, treating him like a mature young man, not a boy. "Learning comes in all forms," Pa claimed, "and knowledge of these town workings is as vital as life itself."

When Adam jumped into his grandfather's buggy, he and his grandfather took off into the evening. Folding his arms across his chest, Adam settled in. As usual, they would talk about the meeting and then would slide right off into the topic of fishing, his favorite subject. He shifted, eyeing his grandfather's strong profile.

"Grandpa, doesn't Dottie's group need a man to help with heavy chores?"

"Sure, they do. That's pretty smart of you. I suppose, once Dottie gets it organized, she'll need some volunteer group. Why do you ask? You want to help?"

"I could."

"I could, too. How about we let her know and get at least, oh, maybe twenty men to help out? Remember what your momma is always saying? 'Many hands make light work.' "

When the horse's soft clip stilled before the first stop sign, Adam concentrated on the smell of the fall leaves as they began to break down in their musty display of odors. For some reason, he loved that smell. He was also thinking of the clop of the horse's hoofs and the wooden wheels. Moments like this, well, life was just perfect.

A truck's lights flared down the street, the glare focusing toward them. Since it passed the last telephone pole before he could blink, it must be going over fifty miles per hour, but why was the truck holding most of the road?

Whoosh! It swiped their horses, and everything went tumbling in the air. Adam landed hard on his shoulder, bumped his head, and crunched some fingers. Feeling no other pain, he eased himself up, looking for his grandfather.

In the darkness, the taste of dirt and grit clogged his mouth. Blood thrummed through his head, the noise almost blocking the people yelling. As he lifted himself up, a tight-fisted man stomped toward him. The noise, the yelling hurting Adam's head, came from him. *Why is he so angry?* The man moved as if he would walk right up and punch Adam in the face.

"You stupid people!" the man growled and then spit out more foul language. He stopped, towering over Adam as he palmed a cell phone, complaining to someone about some country hicks pulling out in front of him.

But that wasn't true! Adam scanned the area for his grandfather. There, he lay crumpled by the sidewalk. Adam stumbled toward him a step, but the cursing man grabbed him and yanked him close, demanding if he was okay. Adam could only nod, even though he didn't know. The pungent scent of alcohol fogged over him, and the stream of cursing intensified the thrumming in his head to a throbbing. He wriggled from the man's grip and scrambled to his grandfather. His grandfather's left leg twisted back, bleeding. A lot.

With all the confusion around them, his grandfather peered deep into Adam's eyes and smiled. He reached over for Adam's hand. As Adam grasped those cold fingers, his gaze fell to his grandfather's stomach. Sticking out from it was a metal signpost.

"Don't touch it, Adam," Grandpa warned, still so calm.

Adam looked back into his grandfather's eyes, and as if those eyes had hands with which to hold, they locked strongly onto Adam's. He couldn't turn away. His grandfather was smiling. He kept smiling at Adam while rubbing his hand with his thumb.

"Sing with me, Adam." He spoke in the darkness.

"What?"

" 'Just Give Me Jesus.' It has been in my head all day." Then his grandfather in his low bass tone started to sing, " 'In the morning, when I rise…' "

Adam tried to sing. But his throat felt hard, and he was crying, so only a few words at a time would come out. But his grandfather sang on. He came to the last stanza:

" 'And when I come to die,

" 'And when I come to die

" 'And when I come to die,

" 'Give me Jesus,

" 'Give me Jesus,

" 'Give me Jesus,

" 'You can have this entire world, just give me Jesus.' "

He sang low but strong, never wavering at all, smiling, looking deep into Adam's eyes. And when he was done, he was gone.

CHAPTER 6

HE WAS A MAN OF DECISION

A warm sun held the sky above them when they all gathered at the grave site to say goodbye to Gilson Troy Stands. All the fall colors lit the day even brighter than it began. When everyone tightened together, they numbered over two hundred. Since there were so many of them, Preacher Tom directed a group of men to bring a wagon, close to the end row. There, he climbed up onto the old wagon, so all could hear him. Having known Grandpa Gill for over thirty years, Preacher Tom was well qualified to say what was proper and due for his graveside speech. But, who would have thought, it would be a life-changing lesson?

"I want to thank you all for coming to Gill's burying. We are not sending Gill off to go to Heaven, because if you knew Gill, you would know he is already in the arms of Jesus. I have come to pay my respect to a man who was well known for the *decisions* he made in his life.

"Gilson Stands… you could say he was a kind man, a good neighbor, strong, wise, gentle, God-fearing, and God-loving. But you could only say all these things because of the *decisions* he made. He told me once, when he was fourteen years old, he was sitting on a fence in the summer field, looking out at the glory of its beauty. And there he began to think about his family and all he had learned of God the Father. On that simple fence, Gill gave his life to God and asked Jesus to forgive him of his sins. He didn't have cancer to get him to that place. He didn't have anything bad pushing at him to make that choice. He just decided God was good and he wanted to live with Him, not against Him.

"Later on in life, he was known for the *decision* of marrying his wife, Mary Lou, and then deciding what kind of husband he would be to her, what kind of father he would be to his children and his grandchildren, what kind of neighbor he would be to all of you. Yes, Gill…"

As the preacher spoke, Adam's tears flowed. He clenched his fists, thinking of Grandpa Gill singing to him while he was dying. Grandpa also had made that *decision*, and it had been a good one.

When Preacher Tom finished, soft sniffles murmured from the women around Adam, while the men peered forward, stoic expressions accompanying affirming nods. He concluded by letting them all think about the *decisions* they had or hadn't made in their lives.

When it came to the point where Adam was to take his place to drop a flower onto his grandfather's silvery casket, he stopped, squatted, bowed his head, and prayed. He first made sure that Jesus was his savior; he wanted it to be clear to himself. Next, while he was praying, he thought of the man who had killed Grandpa Gill and added, "God, I will never let liquor or foul language *ever* pass my lips!"

And with that, he made the *choice* to become a man of his own *decisions.*

CHAPTER 7

THE MEETING

As time kept marching on, what man had built jeopardized the safety of the world. The world was out of control. Danger created by gas fires, excess pressure, or downed power lines had to be addressed. Man didn't want to shorten his lifespan any further than what he was already facing. Experts were assigned to handle these dangerous situations by shutting down gas mains, power plants, dams, and biohazard compounds, plus more. Everywhere man turned, he had to clean up, shut off, or empty out something that could cause him to be poisoned, blown up, or drowned.

Adding to the chaos was the problem of the evil people. Yes, they still existed. You'd think by now they would get it, but no, they became worse —more angry, self-centered, and lazy. If shouting wouldn't get them what they wanted, a bullet could. They abused the mentally handicapped by making them work for them; they took from the poor and elderly, never looking back. Alongside them were the party-till-you-die folks. Always waiting to be talked into any hedonistic idea, they actively left trails of tears and pain where they thought they'd discover trails of happiness.

Four more years of this constant change came and went, and the population continued to dwindle. Those who understood it was God's doing took Him seriously and were much happier for it. Others made the way harder for most as they still enjoyed sin as a delicious dish.

After some time, different areas did start to observe some settling down. The city dwellers had grouped off into smaller towns, ones appealing more to their lifestyles. What factories were still running were making items like toilet paper. Maybe because sixteen years had passed, they had become used to there being no more children. Maybe it was because they had aged. But areas were calming down. People didn't live with their fingers so tightly on the trigger. Yet they kept their guns loaded.

The Stands family continued working their farm and remaining fairly self-sufficient. All the children had married by now, except young Adam. The extended families united as one to work the two-hundred-acre farm, except the oldest son, Dan. He was a doctor, and his wife, Kally, assisted as his nurse.

Adam had become more muscular and rugged from the farm work but never lost his gentle smile. When he would start talking, his face would be bright, with almost a chuckle behind it, as though he took delight in what others were saying. And those sweet eyes seemed to calm people when he looked at them. He heeded his parents and was content. Yes, that was the word you could use for Adam—content.

On February 28, Adam's father called the family together for one of their frequent family meetings. These often took place when they needed to discuss farm business or help someone out in need. But tonight's meeting was to be one most important to all of them.

"Hey, Grandma Stands, may I sit by my best girl?" Adam asked as he approached his grandmother sitting on the couch. The living room in this farmhouse was old-fashioned for their modern day. An old crank phone decorated one wall, while shelves with laced teacups depicted Marlene's sweet personality.

A cute, spunky woman, who loved her grandkids almost as much as she loved God himself, Grandma Stands was always the kind of person to join in their fun—if she didn't start it in the first place. Teasing him back, she patted the couch and proceeded to charge him a nickel just to sit next to her, which he paid. Then she linked her arm in his.

Adam leaned back. No one had said what tonight's topic was. He smiled, peace surging through him as his older siblings and their spouses came in chatting and hugging. Love for them warmed him—love and appreciation for their love. Even though they lived right next door to each other, this was their typical way of greeting each other. Grandma and Grandpa Clip, his mother's parents, settled onto the opposite sofa. Three sets of aunts and uncles, as well as a couple of close cousins, crammed the farmhouse living room, some standing, some sitting on the braided rug. Finally, when his pa and mom came out of the kitchen, his pa took center stage.

"Good evening, family. I'm glad to see you all were able to make it. After we have our meeting tonight, Marlene has set up some refreshments in the kitchen, so you can have something to chew on besides tonight's topic. Let us first join in prayer and ask the Good Lord to give us wisdom." He closed his eyes and lowered his head.

Adam reached for his grandmother's hand as the family chained together for prayer. A moment to him that portrayed a sweetness more than the freshly baked cinnamon buns waiting over in the kitchen.

"God," Pa spoke, "when we share tonight, please guide each and every one of us here to what You want for him or her, not letting it be our map, but Yours, amen."

He took a breath, cleared his throat, and began again, "Well, Marlene and I have been talking about this for the past couple of weeks and about these cold winters we've been having. This last winter, being as bad as it was has us focusing on a certain subject. We are finding the years a little harder and harder to contend with."

He waved a hand as if the protests already started.

"Oh, not that we can't handle it, but we are getting older. Plus, we've been thinking about the future of others in this family."

With that, some glanced over at Adam and his siblings. He knew the talk and whispers that followed him and his siblings to a humanless future.

"So Marlene and I have been putting our prayers to God, asking Him to guide us to solutions we can't see. Then the answer we prayed for, we think came in an unexpected letter the other day."

Reaching in his shirt pocket, he removed a letter along with his reading specks. Then he cleared his throat and began. " 'Dear Mr. and Mrs. Stands. With a saddened heart, I am sending you these papers from the deceased Edward J. Sutton. He passed away January 18 of this year."

"Oh, I remember him!" an uncle exclaimed.

One of the aunts added, "Aww, he passed away. What about Mrs. Sutton?"

Pa waited for them to quiet down, then continued. " 'The details are in this pink envelope from my wife. In Ed's will, he left you all of his property and possessions. You can come at any time and inspect all that is yours.' " He glanced around as if he were reading his family's faces.

Then he continued. " 'I have been paid up for a year in advance, to be sure this property and the animals on it are taken care of till you or a family member can come. A copy of the will, a report of the farm, a count of the animals, and a description of the house are also included in Envelope B." He held that part up and finished the letter.

" 'If you could respond as soon as possible, it would be much appreciated. Looking forward to hearing from you, Hank B. Camp.' "

Pa lowered the letter, his eyes meeting Adam's gaze before he removed his glasses and scanned the others facing him again. Rubbing the bridge of his nose, he took a deep breath and added, "Now I know you all can remember Ed and Honey. Ed wrote many times about how he loved the huge place he inherited down there. He claimed it was big enough for us if we wanted to come and live with them on the farm." As he lowered his voice, it sounded more like he already decided. "Marlene and I never considered it—till now."

Adam's heart rate sped up. Inside him, an excitement of a life change even changed his breathing. The eyes of the others in the room around him widened. But no one interrupted.

"Mr. Camp sent us plans of the house and other buildings. This house has seven bedrooms, three baths, a huge kitchen, and a dining room. Plus, a large family room and office. Ed and Honey only used the family room, the kitchen, and one bedroom. I figure it may need some work here and there. But the property also holds a chicken house, sheds, and two barns—one for cattle and such, the other for equipment." Stopping at that point, Pa walked over to Mom and kissed her cheek, then reached around her shoulder, squeezing it. "There are a total of three hundred and fifty acres of good soil. You can guess by now what we are thinking."

Adam's heart paused. No one uttered a sound. His eyes were open to everyone and everything in the room, but his mind was locked somewhere, in hope and growing excitement. He smiled.

"The weather is warmer down there with a longer growing season. It won't take as much work for heating in the winter, the summers will be hotter, but one must give up one thing for another." Tears of small glitter pulled in his eyes. "This town has always been a good place to raise a family. The folks here are some of the best Christians." He choked as his voice stumbled, and he had to clear his throat again. Placing the letter back in his pocket, he signaled the end.

By then both Pa and Mom's eyes held tears—they were probably thinking about their dear friends or even those in the cemetery on the hill. "Now here are Marlene's and my thoughts. We figure Adam and I should go on down, inspect it, take care of business one way or another. Since we've been praying for a door to open up, we must investigate this one. But our wish is for all of you also to pray and ask God if you should come with us. The floor is open for any questions."

No one moved. Each person deep in his or her own thoughts.

Adam leaned forward and braced his elbows on his knees, fingers laced. Then he shifted his gaze from Grandma Stands, to his pa. "When are we to leave?"

"With the weather being quiet right now, I'm hoping as soon as possible."

"That's fine for your family, Jon," one of the cousins spoke up. "But what are you saying to the rest of us?"

"I am sorry, Abe. I should have been clearer." Reaching for one of Marlene's cinnamon rolls, he took a bite, then nodded his head as he swallowed. Then, as if he were delivering a present, he lifted his arms and exclaimed, "Marlene and I are suggesting we all could move there. The house is a big one, and yet we could build other places for everyone right there in one spot. We all could care for one another, help one another. Yes, we know it's too soon for any real answers. And Adam and I need to check this place out. We will come back with a report."

"Well, I would like to come along—if that's okay?" Grandpa Clip folded his arms across his barrel chest. "I'd like to see this place for myself. Mom could stay with Marlene till we come back. What do you think?"

"Sure, and if anyone else wants to come, come. You're all welcome. There's plenty of room in our van, and if you need time to prepare, we can adjust."

While they talked among themselves, no one else felt led to go. The men agreed to stay back and tend things for Pa and Grandpa, and plans to move Grandma's things over and delegate the farm chores started the next discussion.

They were going? Leaving the farm for a trip down South? Adam shifted in his seat, his gaze caught up by Grandma Stand's twinkling eyes.

She jabbed him with a bony elbow. "Well, don't you look as excited as a pup with a new toy?"

He had to laugh as his mind moved so quickly from one thought to another that he couldn't define what was happening in it. He'd heard nothing of the discussion around him as he sat there packing in his thoughts.

CHAPTER 8

CAREFUL, LITTLE EYES, WHAT YOU SEE

Two days later, Adam stilled as his pa knocked on his bedroom door. "Hey, son, are you about ready?"

"Sure, Pa, come on in."

"Well." Eyes twinkling, Pa nodded toward a bulging knapsack. "I know you know how to pack, but…"

"Come on, Pa." Adam chuckled, trying to zip it shut. "Who saved the day when we went camping last time? When we needed the extra tools to fix the boat? And when you and Dave had wet socks, whose knapsack did you guys raid?"

"Yours," came his pa's calm reply. But, from his creased brows, he was already deep in thought as he crossed to the window.

Adam stilled his zipper battle, reading the nostalgia in his pa's expression as he peered out the second-floor bedroom window. Was he thinking of when they were little? Regretting the thought of leaving? "Pa?"

Pa gave a slight shudder and spun back.

"Here, take a look at this." He handed Adam a folded map. "I have a map of each state out in the van, but this one has all the states, and I think you should be in charge of it." Opening the map, he laid it on the unused part of Adam's desk. He pointed at where they lived now and then down the main roads.

Adam smiled. True to form, his pa had marked the town to which they were going.

"The government main road is a straight shot down, and then when we get to this exit here, Tipperville will be only five miles east. We should make it to the farm in eight or nine hours, if all goes well." Still appearing in deep thought, he added, "I have no idea what these towns are like around the area."

When he paused, he looked at Adam so long Adam couldn't face another one of those heartbreaking looks, so he leaned further over the map.

"Someday, when…" His father stopped and shook his head. "Well, where the cities…" He rubbed his temple, brown hair rippling over his hand, then huffed. "Face it, Adam. It will come in handy someday to know what it was once like. You'll have to know where the nuclear plants were, so those areas can be avoided."

Adam bit the inside of his cheek. He couldn't relate to the future that lay far ahead. But he did know his pa had spoken wisdom, and he respected and trusted it.

"Pa, thanks, and I'll remember it."

His pa grabbed the duffle bag, and Adam grabbed the map and a pillow. Then they both headed downstairs. Kisses, hugs, and last words of advice passed around their warm, old kitchen. Marlene and her mom had packed enough food in the van to last for days. The well-kept engine whirred to life, sunlight glinting on the fresh-scrubbed windshield and the farm shrinking in the mirror as they headed to the freeway.

After only a few minutes on the road, Grandpa Clip slapped his hand on the dashboard. "I gotta say it. Jon, I brought along my .45—not that I think we're going to need it, but one can't tell nowadays. I hope you don't mind?"

Adam snapped his gaze to his father's reflection in the rearview mirror, hoping they wouldn't have to turn around to take it back. His pa's soft chuckle drifted through the van.

"No, not at all, Dad. I brought my .22 along. The times are still calling for them, from what I'm hearin'."

"With that off my chest..." Grandpa's cheeky grin emerged. "Let's have a prayer."

Adam bowed his head and waited for one of them to start. But neither said anything, so he unhooked his seat belt, leaned between the two front seats, and put a hand on both.

"Jesus, You sure work in ways we don't understand sometimes, but this trip, we know, is Your directing. So as we travel to this new place, please help us to do Your will while we're gone. Thanks for watching over Mom, Grandma, and the rest of our family and our friends, too. Please, let us know Your will when we get there. We ask this in the name of Jesus, amen."

"Amen," echoed the other men.

"Did you feel that, Dad?" Adam's pa nearly whispered.

Grandpa raised a brow. "What, Jon?"

Pa's gaze flickered to Adam's briefly in the rearview. "Like the anointing just fell on my son."

No one responded. But something warm filled Adam's heart, and he straightened his spine and shoulders as if trying to make himself worthy of his father's words.

As they went along the snowy roads, the yellow, white, and green triangle-in-triangle signs guided the travelers to places with food or gasoline. Red with white and a medical sign demarked anything from dental to hospital. And, now and then, the black-and-white crossbones warned of danger areas; those could symbolize anything. Shuddering, Adam didn't care to know what they represented.

After four hours of changing terrain and one needed gas stop, they came across billboards they couldn't avoid, promoting an unwanted town up ahead. Lining each side of the roadway were signs of porn, signaling to all who drove along, "Come be with us in Little but Big Sin City." With each sign was as even larger photo. For three miles, the signs stood their posts crying out. Adam was told to read a book or look down till they passed. Grandpa and Pa kept their focus only on the road. One sign even stated, "This is what we worship! God don't care."

"I don't get it, Pa. How can people be like that? Do they hate God or just not know Him?"

His pa took a second to answer. Maybe because he was shaken from what had seen. Or maybe he was ashamed of and angry about what he'd exposed his son to. "First, son, when we pass this area, check the mile marker and write it down. We can calculate it backward because we don't want your mom or anyone else to see them. We'll also be able to warn other drivers of this area, so they can keep their eyes on the road. Next, I don't know the reasons people want to live like that. Some are tricked and caught up in it like a spider in a web; some don't know any better, some out of bitterness. But, whatever the reason, when people are lovers of themselves in their world, anything goes."

"Face it"—Grandpa Clip shifted in his seat to look directly at Adam—"there are those who just plain desire evil. God protect us from them. Let me ask you something straight out. How do you feel now, seeing those pictures? Don't answer, boy! Because I will answer it for you. You're feelin' kind of creepy, even dirty. People can't take those photos out of their minds once they have seen them—ever! But my warning is—don't dwell on them. Men have a recall, there in their minds." He tapped his temple. "It's so powerful they can bring it up, at any old time, again and again."

He twisted further in his seat, his wise old eyes latching onto Adam with overwhelming kindness. "If you play that game in your mind, you will lose. It is sin, and it wants every man and woman, not just some. That is why those people have become what they are."

The van was quiet for a long time as if they were concentrating on the light snow flurries floating around as they drove. Finally, Adam sat back and sighed. "Thanks, Grandpa."

Pa glanced over at the wise, outspoken old man and smiled. "Yeah, thanks."

CHAPTER 9

WHERE HAS ALL THE MONEY GONE? OR HAS IT?

As they rode along, so many new sights passed before him. "Whoa!" He scooted forward when a billboard, whitewashed with big black letters stated, "Stay out! No room left in this town! You will be shot!"

"Yeah." Grandpa's lips wrinkled up as sunlight and shadow flickered through the windows. "I like the cute welcoming ones better. Did you see that one a couple of miles back? 'No place to stay? You can jump in our hay!'" He chortled, winking in the rearview.

"I liked 'Momma's always cook'n extra.'" Pa grinned.

Adam settled back, but he didn't mention the one stuck in his mind. The one that still announced, with a weird sense of humor, "Children eat for free!"

On each road sign or building front, a government emblem or emblems specified what type or types of payment were accepted.

The first was a dollar sign, which meant they still took cash, but cash only. That had started when the dollar value had begun to crash. But how could they still be accepting money?

Wealthy men had noted that their wives still wanted things—things they were used to getting—and saw no reason why they had to do without. If the wife wanted her hair done, Jacque was who she wanted to do it. Jacque needed supplies, so he still paid a company for them. The company, in turn, paid cash to its employees for the work needed. The employees needed food they couldn't grow, so they went to the farmers market. The farmer took the money home to the little woman, who sneaked off to get her hair done by Jacque. Thus, money wasn't not dying off as fast as one expected. In fact, money continued to be the circle that united the community.

Next was the second group, who also needed and wanted material goods. The government emblem for them was two hands shaking because bartering was their preferred way. They preferred it because they were good at it. They would size up what one had, then what they wanted, and then the games would begin. Ultimately, the needy one would lose something precious in the transaction. One gained because the other's need left him vulnerable. The winner then took his bartered prize home to his wife and allowed his wife to get her hair done by bartering it to Jacque. Jacque always won. Women just couldn't do without Jacque.

CHAPTER 10

SO WHAT DOES SHE SELL?

The three arrived at the cozy town of Tipperville at approximately, according to their stomachs, dinnertime. As Adam scanned the clean sidewalks with, thankfully, no signs of snow, he hoped this little town still had a nice restaurant for a hot meal. A gentleman in a tan jacket walking with three dogs raised his hand to gesture a hello. Horse-pulled buggies clopped along, and a few cars also lingered.

At the center of the half-mile stretch, Grandma's Place beckoned in gold and black letters on old storefront glass.

Pa pulled over to the open space along the curb. "Let's see if someone in this old store can help us, or we can walk up and down and ask a few people for some information."

"Anything sounds good as long as I can stretch my legs." Adam popped open the van's sliding back door and breathed in air not tainted with road dust.

"True enough." Grandpa sniggered, climbing down from the front. "It looks inviting, and maybe we'll find a restroom."

Grandpa fell back as Pa tried the doorknob. The front door creaked open, and a small tinkle of a bell greeted them.

"Um…" Adam jolted backward, his face heating as if he'd walked right into someone's home, the very living room to be exact. In one smooth move, Pa and Grandpa also turned back, looking at the door they'd entered, obviously thinking they'd been mistaken.

But that's when *she* rounded a corner. "Welcome, gentlemen. How may I help you?" She stood five feet tall with grayed and faded blonde hair, wiping her hands on a red-and-white checked dish towel.

"Well, ma'am." Pa hesitated. "We are sorry—we certainly didn't mean to intrude. Uh, we've just arrived in town and will be heading over to the Sutton place. But we were hoping, since we've come from Ohio, to find a place for some hot food. If you could direct us to a restaurant, if the town still has one, we would much appreciate it."

Adam almost chuckled seeing Pa standing there, shoulders up and chin tucked down like a little boy about to get reprimanded. But Adam's own ears were still heated over having walked into the lady's house.

She looked at them as if sizing them up. "Why are you heading there?"

"To a restaurant, ma'am?"

"No, dear, to the Sutton place."

"It's like this, dear lady." Grandpa Clip filled in Pa's openmouthed silence. "This is my son-in-law." He pointed toward Pa with his hat. "He has inherited the Sutton place, so we've come down here to check on it. But we didn't mean to barge into your home," he added, waving his hat to the wide of the room. Was his neck a bit red, too?

She chuckled. "You must be the Stands."

"Yes, ma'am." Pa's shoulders loosened, and Adam's stomach unknotted, feeling a little better since she knew their names. "How do you know about us?"

"Oh, Ed and Honey always shopped here, and this being a small town, most shop here at Grandma's." She smiled. "For a time here and time there."

"If you don't mind me asking, ma'am"—Adam stepped forward—"what is it you sell?" All he could see was a nice, cozy living room with a wood stove, an extended old-fashioned open kitchen, and a couple of doors. A single sign rested on a coffee table, next to some S-shaped cookies, and it said, "You May Take Two."

"Well, before I explain, let me invite you in. God has led you to the right place, so don't worry about finding somewhere to eat." She started toward the kitchen as she spoke as if she expected them to follow, and they did.

"Now, the Good Lord had me cook a lot of extra food tonight. Goodness knows I could never eat this much." Turning her back to them, she talked as she was opening a drawer. "So, don't think this strange, but from what I know about you Stands, you already know how God works. See the door over there?" She pointed with a spoon. "It goes to the privy. Now, you can go and wash up. When you come back, you can help by settin' the table."

They looked at each other, smiled, shrugged, and then did as they were told. When they came back, Adam took charge of the silverware, Pa the plates, and Grandpa the cups of coffee and milk.

In front of them now beckoned beef stew, cornbread, and fresh salad, a meal fit for a king. When they sat, the old woman clasped the hands on either side of her. Together, they bowed their heads while she spoke. "Well, Father, You got them here okay, and we thank You for that. This food You provided to be cooked up beforehand was just the cherry on top. I needed this miracle more than their bellies. Yes, I thank You for this food, and I know You have already blessed it, and in our hearts, we thank You for that also. It is in Jesus' name that we've prayed this prayer, amen."

They all repeated, "Amen."

"Now, dig in, and I'll answer the first question young Adam asked. What is it I sell here? Let's see, I have been in business here for almost ten years. My husband and I had to open the store because my Bill messed up his back taking care of our hogs. We turned to God for an answer since my Bill's back was not getting any better. Then God gave both of us a dream of starting up this business. So, we sold our home to some city folks who were moving down here, and we opened this place." She nodded her head once and sat back.

Adam glanced at Grandpa, cocking an eyebrow and squinting, and, of course, Grandpa jumped in. "That sounds great! So, what is it you ended up selling?"

"Ah…" She winked. "That is the point: neither of us wanted to sell anything or had any business training at our age, so we agreed to sell nothing."

Pa tilted his head. "You sell *nothing*?"

"Exactly, and we've sold a lot of it. And, I am glad to report, this is one of the few businesses in town that's still doing well." She then proceeded to eat.

Leaning forward, Adam blew out air and chuckled. "I don't get it. How can you sell nothing and make a living at it? Further, you claim to have customers, lots of them."

She finished chewing, took a sip of her coffee, and patted her mouth, then smiled his way. "Oh, we can't take any credit for it. The whole thing was God's idea. He told us to do it."

She leaned forward, and almost without knowing it, so did Adam. "Bill and I were just as confused as you are. God tellin' us to open a shop and to sell nothing—mind you, I wasn't complaining because it sounded like a lot less work."

She snorted a giggle out as she shook her head.

"Think about it: no stock, nothing to make, nothing to break or spoil. But this is the secret of what God wanted us to do: He told us we were to offer to all who walked in this door a *gift of hospitality* and represent Him. And then, it is up to the people if they want some or not. We put no price on it, offering someone a place to sit or to have a cookie for the stomach, a place to read with a cup of coffee or tea."

His stew finished, Adam sipped his coffee. Rich and strong, it glided over his tongue, perhaps the best he'd had in years.

"Soon after opening, this place took on a life of its own. People stopped in to eat their packed lunches. Some came in for a place to sit or for answers. One person set up a puzzle, and since then, puzzles have always been part of the room. Can you understand now? The people in the town or those passing through come in here all the time for something, and God with His love wants to serve them."

Grandpa eased aside his bowl and folded his arms on the table before him, his eyes twinkling and lips edging up in a smile.

And the little lady gave a firm nod, dipping her pointy chin down. "People have laughed, cried, and made the Good Lord their Savior in this little shop. We have never asked for money in any way. But people started dropping off things as gifts—milk here, wood there. Bill and I have never lacked anything. In fact, we have gotten more than what we could use, so when that happens, we pass it along, back to the people."

Just as she paused, the front door jingled. A young man walked right into the kitchen and greeted them. "Hi, Grandma. Good evening, folks." He then proceeded to retrieve a glass from the cupboard and head to the fridge for milk.

"Do you need any dinner tonight, Ted? There's plenty."

"No thanks, Grandma. After I read a few chapters, I'll be headin' over to Ma's. She'll be expecting me."

"Well, the garbage needs to be taken out tonight. Please don't forget."

"No problem."

From where Adam was sitting, he could see Ted plop himself down on the couch, use a coaster for his milk, grab a book at the side table, and bite into a cookie. Adam tilted his head back to their host. "He's your grandson?"

"Oh no. Ted's been coming here for a couple of months now. Right now, he's in the middle of a good book and likes a place to unwind before he goes home."

"He takes out your garbage?"

"You set the table, didn't you?"

"Point taken."

When this newly bonded team talked through dinner, the travelers learned her beloved Bill had passed on. At the end, they cleared the table, helped with the dishes, and gave thanks to the shopkeeper, promising always to "shop" there.

But, as young Adam started to climb into the van, he asked if he could go back in for a moment. He found her in the kitchen, fixing a cup of tea.

"What is it, Adam?"

"May I call you grandma?"

"Yes, dear. That's what everyone calls me. But that's not what you came back for, is it?"

"No, ma'am. The food you prepared tonight—how did you know God wanted you to make it?"

She giggled, eyes sparkling. "This is how God works. Today, Howard Caswell stopped in. He said he had some extra vegetables for me. Then Helen, a friend of mine, dropped off extra beef for me, but I wasn't home to inform her that my small freezer was full. So, I sat and looked at all this food. I asked God what to do with it. He said, 'Cook it!' And I squashed my eyes and thought: He has something up His sleeve."

Adam's face lit up. "Oh man!"

Smiling, he shook his head and walked to the van, but not before Grandma sat back, sipped her tea, and smiled. "Yeah, God. Oh man!"

CHAPTER 11

THE SUTTON FARM

The sun had already set when they wound up the long drive. Yet, because of a full moon and a clear sky, cattle were visible in the field to the left and horses to the right. Before getting out of the van, they sat, surveying the Sutton farm and listening to the cattle bray as they came closer to the barns, probably curious about the newcomers. The air had cooled to the lower 50s, though it felt as warm as 70 compared to where they came from.

At length, Pa shifted to meet their eyes. "Boys, I don't have a key."

"Well, we shouldn't go trying these windows." Grandpa nodded at them. "Who knows what things might be hiding in all that brush? We can try all the doors and see if there's a key hidden."

They walked around to each door, trying them in hope. As they tried the last one, the clip of a galloping horse echoed up the drive. The rider pulled up closer, but not too close. Stopping in a clear patch of moonlight, he lifted a stern voice. "May I help you?"

A gun straddled the front of the saddle. His right hand rested against the butt.

Pa walked three steps forward. "I am Jon Stands, and I believe I am the new owner of this farm. And you are?"

"Hank Camp. I'm the one who wrote you." Walking his horse closer, Hank sat looser in the saddle now. "I wasn't expecting you folks, and I live across the way. Well, when my dogs bark, I inspect."

"I apologize for putting you through this, Mr. Camp." Pa stretched out his hand. "I should have thought to get a hold of you before we came down."

"Well, it's too late to get up early. First, you can call me Hank, and next, I have a key."

For the next two hours, they toured the large white farmhouse with its so inviting porches and the two massive strong barns that once held more stock than they ever farmed. Hank told them he had been the foreman of the Sutton farm for the last ten years Ed's parents had owned it. The agreement had been made to meet the needs of each family. Adam couldn't help but notice that Hank walked with a strong limp and wonder how he could keep up with the work until he learned Hank had three other men working for him.

As the first night's tour ended, they shook hands and promised to meet in the morning to help with the chores.

Grandpa stood in the kitchen door as Hank got back on his horse and then rode down the drive. "Nice man."

Cupboards squeaked as Adam opened them. He'd lost track of how many. "Mom will just love this kitchen."

"Yep, she definitely will." Pa tried the faucets. "And, looking at all the stuff this place already has, we wouldn't have much to move." He pulled open a drawer, tapped the pots and pans hanging, then grabbed the coffee pot to fill with water. "Ah, this is my favorite. And Ed has a huge bin of coffee. That man did like his coffee."

"Yes, sir." Grandpa whistled. "This kitchen is big enough for all the women to run around in and never bump an elbow."

Catching the wink his grandpa shot his way, Adam chuckled.

"Yep, but ya know, Jon, as soon as Marlene hears about three big, screened-in porches, she'll never hear or care about anything else."

"You'll never guess what I like." Adam strode to the side sink. "I love this hand pump." He touched the red pump and pumped the arm up and down till out ran cool, clear water. "Case the well pump stops, you still can have your coffee."

"If there still is coffee," grumbled Grandpa.

"Let's not go there tonight." Pa lowered his gaze and rubbed the back of his neck.

They talked for a while longer, unloaded the van, and then picked out their rooms for the night.

In the morning, Adam volunteered to go out looking for fresh eggs, an excuse to check around the farm in the daylight. A shed on small stilts rested next to the chicken coop. Before going back with his collection of eggs, he could take one peek at that shed. As he turned the lock, a wood piece on a nail, and looked inside the newly lit room, his heart leaped in his chest. He leaned forward in the doorway, craning to see what else awaited inside. It took every bit of his strength not to enter, but he pulled himself together and headed back up to the house.

The kitchen screened door slammed behind him as he entered. Apparently, Mr. Camp had just arrived because he was still holding a box, which he passed to Adam. Before placing it on the table, Adam inhaled the sweet aroma of fresh hot cinnamon rolls.

"Man, this day can't get any better! First, I find a treasure out in the shed next to the chickens and then this."

"Hank, this is much appreciated. Tell your missus she made our day." Pa removed a homemade block of butter from the box and headed for the stove. "What's your find, Adam?"

"Fishing equipment galore! I figure, with as much equipment as I saw out there, there has got to be a place to fish. Is there, Mr. Camp?"

"Oh yeah, over in the east pasture is one pond. It connects to a stream running through the back, then lines up to the west fencing. Then, about a half-mile back, on the far-east side, is a good-sized fifty-acre lake that now belongs to you guys. Ed's family always called it Joppa Lake. It butts up to a small part of your neighbors' spread. The people on the other side are a strange bunch, and it is best you stay on your side. But go right ahead and fish because the whole lake belongs to you. Oh, and six miles up the road is Crab Lake. It's a good size, also."

For the next two days, they worked the farm along with Hank and the crew. On and off in the daytime, they took notes for Marlene of what was in each closet, drawer, and room. The less they had to haul, the better.

Marlene and her mother were doing about the same thing. Even though they had not been given the go-ahead, they were going from room to room to see what could be left or taken. Some family heirlooms made the list to go with them while they kept a second list of things to give to friends. Having decided to tackle the attic, Marlene gathered her notepad, and her mother followed.

"These stairs are getting to my knees." Her mother pulled up on the handrail to help ease the strain.

"Oh, you don't have to come up, Mom, if you don't want to." Marlene paused and touched her mother's arm. "It's just the attic."

Her mother brushed her off with a hand tsk. "This will be the hardest room of all. Most of the time, whatever is stacked up in an attic is something you just couldn't part with."

As the two proceeded up the creaky steps, Marlene shivered. She'd forgotten how cold it would be up there. So she had to prop open the door so the lower heat could find its way up. After she made them a place to sit, they began to go through the old brittle cardboard boxes. "Good gracious, Marlene. Why on earth did you save this?" Her mother held up an old lampshade with a big rip in its side.

Marlene leaned forward, squinting at the dusty old form, mouth pursed. Then her lips turned into a goofy grin while her eyebrows still clamped together. "I have no idea!" Still studying the yellowed old ripped lampshade, she pressed a hand to her chest. "Maybe, just maybe, I thought…" She sat back and shrugged her shoulders, laughing. "Honestly, I have no idea what I was thinking."

Each item had a history along with a precious story, unlike the unwanted lampshade. Until they pulled all the saved baby things, it quieted down, and the laughing came to a halt. Marlene lifted each item, smelling it first as if she was looking for one more precious fragrance of her tiny cooing babies.

"I can't bring myself to throw them out, Mom. I don't have it in me." She held it close to her chest. "And I know I can't take them with us."

She picked up another cute little outfit. She turned it left and right, brought it to her nose again.

"I know, dear. I feel the same. I hear some of the women have been taking a lot of the baby things over to elementary schools and storing them there."

Marlene shook her head. "Nah, I can't take these things there and leave them. I never even sent my kids there. Why would I take their baby things there?"

Her mother folded up an old baby blanket, but not before she smelt it and hugged it. "Let's leave them for now. Who knows? Maybe there will be some room when we go."

"If we go," Marlene reminded her mom.

CHAPTER 12

THE NINE

Jon drove his son and father-in-law into town two days before they were going to head home. First, he wanted to meet up with Grandma at Grandma's Place, to let her know they'd decided to move down and also to leave her gifts to help keep her store supplied with kindness. Next, he planned to walk over to the small country store a block down the street to call his oldest son and let the family know of their plans.

The man in the tan jacket meandered toward them. He hadn't that cheerful bounce now, and he wasn't walking three dogs, but two. As they approached, a pang shot through Jon. The man's face drooped, and bloodshot eyes peered vacantly from puffy lids.

Hesitating even to say hello, for it might increase this man's troubles, but not being able to stop a natural reaction, he reached out an extended hand. "Hello, sir. I'm Jon Stands, and this is my son, Adam, and my father-in-law, Ron Clip."

"Good afternoon," answered the older gentleman with a voice as low as his demeanor. Without offering any more information, he walked on.

But Grandpa stepped around and tapped the man's shoulder. "I'm sorry for whatever you're going through, sir. It's something rough. Is there *anything* we can do to help?"

The man stopped and stared at them with a blank face. Then he spat his words. "I hope you are not going to be like those... those... The Nine and respect what belongs to others. There's no call to kill an innocent, even if it is just a dog!"

The man's eyes let out a flood of tears. His mouth contorted to a shaky frown as he tried to reach in his pocket for a hanky.

Jon cupped a hand on the old man's shoulder, feeling he should be on his guard in case the man collapsed while his son scooted down to pet the dogs when, as if they were in tune with their master's grief, they started to whine.

The exhausted man wiped his still leaking eyes with shaking hands and a tear-streaked handkerchief. "I'm sorry. I know you aren't those others. But, right now, my heart is still breaking for my dog, and my anger is still at a hot boil."

Jon gave the man's shoulder a gentle squeeze. "May I ask what's happened, sir? If you can't talk about it, I understand." *But who are these The Nine that could make an old man cry like this?*

"Well, I hate to report this if you don't already know, but they're your neighbors."

"What?" A jolt shot through him. "This doesn't sound like something I want to hear." He lowered his hand and held the man's gaze. "But I need to know. We *were* planning to move here."

The older man told them he needed to sit down and pointed to a bench in front of the store. Jon walked him over to sit. When he was on the bench, the older man sniffed, blew his nose, and readjusted his hands around the leashes of the two dogs. Man's best friends sat and then snuggled up to their master. One was sitting on his feet, and both were looking up at him. Putting one hand on the back of one's head, he patted the other's.

"Yeah." He had to clear his throat and began again. "Your neighbors aren't what this town wants to live here. They came from up north a year ago. They just took over the Oldster farm. See, the Oldsters were a nice older couple, but when The Nine went up to the farm, as they tell it, they found the Oldsters sick. At least, that's what The Nine said. They also said the Oldsters gave them the whole place—lock, stock, and barrel—and passed away, all in one day. Though, with a story like that, no one in town believed them."

Grandpa Clip planted his foot on the bench and leaned an elbow on his knee. "Why do you keep calling them 'The Nine?' "

The old man kept petting his dogs as they kept panting and smiling their dog smiles. "It's what they call themselves, and there are nine of them. I heard, before they came here, they were some kind of music band, and The Nine was their name."

The old man sighed. "Yesterday, the bunch of them was horsing around all over town on their motorcycles, till one of them ran out of gas right in front of my place. They walked to the back of our home. I was back there, tending to my chickens, and the one they call Grizzly—he was acting tough and using a ton of lousy language—yelled at me to get him some gas. I wasn't going to put up with that. I told them to get off my property."

He rolled his shoulders and shook his head, a tremor running through his whole body. "They got nastier and nastier, demanding I get the gas. My wife, hearing all the ruckus outside, opened the back door to see what was going on. And one of the women walked up and pushed her inside. She said, 'Let's see what you got cookin' in here, old woman.' That's when my golden lab, Cassie, jumped on her and bit her."

He hung his head and wept again. "One of the other girls grabbed a frying pan and killed our Cassie with one blow. My wife had to witness her still hitting poor Cassie's body and cussing at her. They took what they wanted and left, laughing the whole time."

No one could say a thing, but Jon clenched his jaw. Everything changed with neighbors like that next door. "We are very, very sorry! And we thank you for being able to tell us." Turning to Grandpa, he said, "There is no way I could move here, not with people like that next to my family." He offered the older gentleman a ride home.

Drained of his strength, the man accepted.

"If you don't mind my asking," said Grandpa. "What… about the police? Can't they arrest them for what they did?"

"Oh, I called Terry Barns, he's our state trooper here, but when he went to arrest them, they said it was our word against theirs. That they had gone up to the door to ask for some gas when Cassie attacked them. Terry knew it wasn't true, but the only thing he could do was warn them he wouldn't put up with another similar story. They laughed, made fun like they were innocent and we were guilty." He wiped his nose and pushed to his feet, offering his other hand. "I never did introduce myself. I'm Nathan Tarsh."

CHAPTER 13

IT WENT INTO THE DEPTHS OF ME

Adam drummed his fingers against the nearby plastic armrest as Pa drove them back to the house. They didn't make the phone call up north.

"I can't believe Hank never told us about them," Pa complained as he prepared to fry ham for dinner.

Washing off some potatoes, Grandpa paused, then shrugged. "He did mention to Adam to stay away from them when he was telling him about the back lake."

"Grumpy neighbors are one thing, Dad, but possible murderers and violent thieves are entirely different."

Adam swept a curtain aside. "Well, you'll have your chance to ask him. He's riding up right now."

Grandpa opened the door and greeted Hank, adding it was a good thing he'd come by as they had run into some problems.

"Can I get you some dinner?" Pa asked.

Hank declined, but he helped himself to a cup of coffee. Watching him pour it, Pa folded his arms and rested against the counter. "Well, Hank, I don't know how to put it but to ask you straight out: How come you didn't explain about what kind of neighbors we're up against?"

"Oh boy, what happened? It must be The Nine."

Pa filled him in on Mr. Tarsh's story.

"Jon." Hank rubbed his temple. "I never even thought. I was so caught up with you and your family coming down—and they hadn't been up to anything of late—that, well, they never came to mind."

Grandpa sat down and, after saying grace for them, cut into his ham. "It changes everything, Hank. We can't bring our families down here after what happened to that gentleman and his wife."

"I'm sorry." Hank lowered his head. "I would give anything to have you over The Nine. Now what?"

"First, I don't have to forgive you for anything. You didn't do anything wrong."

Pa was quiet for a bit. "How about we stay a few more days, make arrangements to give the farm to you and to the rest of the guys who have been working it? Maybe that's what God wanted us to do all along, so The Nine can't get their hands on it?"

They spent the evening discussing arrangements. When Hank left, Pa joined Adam on the back porch. In the dark, Pa settled in the comfortably cushioned wicker rocking chair and rocked while Adam leaned against the back wall, listening to the night's inviting sounds, thinking about how much Ma would love it here.

"You okay, Adam?" Pa's voice cracked the silence.

"Nah. Pa, I'm angry inside like Mr. Tarsh. They may not have come up our drive, but they ruined it here for us just the same."

"I know. I'm feeling the same. I may not show it, but it's tough for me also. But you understand why I can't bring Mom and the rest down?"

Adam shook his head. "I wouldn't want them here now, but this place was perfect."

They sat in the dark listening to the noise God provides so the dark wouldn't be empty.

"Hey, I have an idea. We won't be leaving for four more days, and you aren't needed for any chores. So why don't you take the time to do some fishing? Take the equipment out in the shed and put it to use. When we leave, take it back home, but fishing weather won't be as nice as it is now."

The next morning, Adam got up extra early, made his breakfast, packed a lunch, and headed to the inviting shed.

Man, I even love the mornings here. Wearing his rubber boots to walk through the high grass, he followed the directions he'd memorized to the lake.

Minutes later, Joppa Lake glistened in the sunrise. He stood awhile, looking at it. The calm of the water reflected the trees. Rocks settled here and there, posting points of fishing interest. At the water's edge, a wooden rowboat, as inviting as cool water to a hot tongue, nestled onshore. Nope, no fishing on land for him today. He went straight for the boat.

He flipped an old tarp off it, revealing a corroding plastic bottle with one side cut out for bailing out water, two oars snug in their locks, and an anchor of rock and firm rope.

As the early sun warmed his back, he bailed out the water and set his tackle box inside. Then, bracing his hands on the bow, he pushed out the floating oasis and jumped in.

He rowed slowly, not only studying the early morning sun but also figuring the right place to drop his line. However, at the same time, his mind started playing with thoughts that he might have to leave this pleasing fishing place. He was also contemplating all he had heard about his neighbors. Trying to kick out the choking thoughts, he readied his reel.

Cast, plunk, reel in… Cast, plunk, reel in… Two healthy-size bass were caught in minutes.

Now, anyone who does any fishing knows problems can arise at any time. Then Adam got himself hooked on something under the water, close to the other shore. *No problem.* He'd gotten out of these before. He paddled over to retrieve it. Since he wasn't able to unhook it, he conceded and broke the line.

As he finished, a jolt coursed through him. A woman stood about thirty-five feet up the shore, watching him as she was stretching. The trees all around the camp had been cut down, stripping the innocent land of its worth. A brown tent staked the ground beside a smoking firepit, with the trash of cans, bottles, and other junk strewn around the ground.

Adam's temper rose again, kindling something inside he'd never dealt with. In his mind, the words swirled: *Now they've even taken this lake from you, too!* All he could think about was what they'd done to the people who lived there, to the old man, to his poor wife, and what she'd had to witness happening to the dog they loved.

As he rowed back to escape the sight of the camp, he heard her yell out, "What you doin', boy? Fishin'? How about you come over here, and we can talk." She laughed as if she had some deep, dark secret.

A thought also came into his head that he should go and tell them about God. *What? Adam, you are losing it. That's like telling a striking rattlesnake about Jesus, and that will never happen. I have better sense than that! If they were looking for God, that would be one thing, but the way they take from others and the sickening cruelty they delight in… they are not looking for God. They are mocking Him.*

He rowed hard to get the other side and farther down, trying not to see them. Even though they were out of sight, a restlessness of hate continued to grow hot inside him. He couldn't concentrate. He found his teeth clenching his jaw tight. Trying to calm himself, he lowered the anchor and reached for his rod and cast another line out. But his mind was already caught up and tangled in hate.

Once more, he could hear them laughing and cursing. Their crude voices traveled with ease across the water, stealing the last of his desired fishing solitude.

Adam threw down his rod, jammed the tackle back into its box, and then leaned over to lift the anchor from its depth to head home. When his eyes beheld *it*.

He had never seen one in his life, but he heard about them and saw them in photos. He didn't understand how it could be, for the sky above was sunny with fluffy white clouds. But even he could tell the monster was approaching maddeningly fast, pushing a wall of thick, black, swirling wind with lightning in its darkness.

His anchor wouldn't budge! He yanked it to the left and then to the right as he kept checking the sky. He grabbed the pocketknife out of his jeans and hacked into the rope, but it had been entwined with wire and strong nylon, making the cutting impossible to do in a short time.

Winds blew hard, now bringing hail and flying debris. Could he swim to shore? The waves rolled, yanking the anchored boat here and there. The angry tunnel now sounded like a roaring train. He had no time.

The boat twisted him to face The Nine. They were running from the camp.

At least you'll die with me, too!

Like a hand, the wind tossed him hard into the angry water, then into the depths of this unknown lake, churning him around so hard he knew no way to the surface.

God, I'm Yours! He released his soul to God in this blackness, hoping God was taking The Nine. When in front of him, he saw light. Kicking off the rubber boots holding him down, he pushed with all his strength.

Coughing, gasping, he broke the surface, finding the winds had now passed. He positioned to swim toward the shore, then stilled, taken aback to discover he was only in a few feet of water, the sandy bottom grating against his knees. He rose, covered with mud, every inch of him heavy with seaweed.

There The Nine stood, not dead or blown away, swearing and assessing themselves. Quieting, they watched him rise from the water.

Imagining he looked something of a swamp creature, with his feet sucking in the mud as he tried to walk, Adam wiped the water from his eyes. It came to him again to speak of God. *Well then, God, You tell me what to say.*

"Tell them of their doom."

Adam squinted in anger and walked toward them, his temper in full force. He screamed his message at them. "God has told me to tell you your lives have been spared for now, but you will be answering to Him soon. Your cruel and wicked ways have added up in His sight like a mountain, and none—He means none—of your wicked deeds will be forgotten. You will be the ones that will be judged as each and every one of your ugly deeds will be uncovered.

"Every day, He sees you nine refusing to turn to Him. You want nothing to do with Him, yet He still waits for you. I don't understand it, but He waits! He wants me to tell you about the Cross. Well, get this: Jesus died on that Cross to rid you of all of your lousy sins. You think it ended there. Jesus may have died for your sins, but He got out of that death on His own to give you the gift you never, ever, *ever* deserved! Hope you have a Bible, folks, 'cause you sure do need one."

With his throat going hoarse from screaming, he stormed toward home.

CHAPTER 14

LET ME SPEAK TO YOUR HEART, SO YOU HAVE A CHOICE

Adam found his adrenaline now gone, leaving his body spent to the point he was unable to work his way back to the house, when suddenly he was relieved to hear his father's voice shouting for him.

But because he was weak, his reply was no louder than a normal speaking tone. "I'm over here." He tried again to raise his voice, but with no success. Exhausted from his temper, the tornado, and the screaming, his body now started to shake so violently he couldn't walk and slumped against a tree.

Pa had been rushing in the direction of the lake, calling out again and again, not knowing if Adam was even alive. When he fell silent, silence rushed in all around, like the land was still holding its breath. In that silence, he stopped and used it to listen until he heard Adam's small voice. "Are you all right? Here, let me help you."

He grabbed Adam as Adam started to collapse to the ground. Ever so slowly, the two made it back to the house.

Pa washed Adam with warm soothing water listening to what had happened, including Adam's confession about screaming at The Nine. Then he shook his head, and in his strong and low voice, he said, "Let it go, son. My advice is just let it go."

Adam fell asleep and slept till noon the next day. Grandpa was there when he woke with a plate of food for him. Adam moved out to the front porch where he sat the rest of the afternoon, replaying what God had told him to say to The Nine until a trail of dust curved up their drive. The setting sun glared, blocking his view of the vehicle until it stopped before the house. A state police car.

Grandpa walked out onto the steps to greet the officer. "Good afternoon, sir. Is everything all right?"

"Good afternoon, folks. I'm Officer Burns. Are you the Stands family?"

"We are, in a way. I'm the grandfather. Ronald Clip is my name, and this is my grandson, Adam Stands."

Burns shook Grandpa Clip's hand and acknowledged Adam. "I've come with an odd request of you folks."

"Oh?" Grandpa cocked his head, lowing his chin to look over his readers. "And what is that?"

"Well, let's see. Your neighbor—Grizzly, the leader of The Nine—was in a motorbike accident last night. He's in Grace Hospital in the next town and asking to see young Adam here."

Adam stiffened. "Why does he want to see me?"

"Not sure, except he says it's real important, and he even said please. I never thought he *knew* that word."

Grandpa Clip slid the van keys from his pocket. "Sure. How do we get there?"

Two hours later, Adam followed Pa and Grandpa into a hospital room already crowded with the rest of The Nine. Grizzly, in bed, displayed a cast-covered leg hung from pulleys. Stitches and tape crisscrossed his left arm. Purple blotched his face—his eye, his cheek, and his jaw so swollen no features remained distinguishable.

But Grizzly smiled, cracking open a scab on his lip. "Thanks for coming."

Adam suppressed a shudder, avoiding the other sullen faces.

"Well"—Grizzly's voice crackled, coming past a low gurgle in his throat—"first, I must tell you that was some speech you gave yesterday. After you left, lookin' like you did, we talked about seeing that tornado thing coming down on you. Where we stood, we saw a dark powerful cloud in the shape of a big black hand reaching right over you. We all tried to take off and get, but the hail and wind was stirring up the dirt and branches with the rain so strong… Well, we couldn't tell which way to go, so the only thing we could do was drop down with no cover." He coughed several times spiting the unclogged phlegm into a paper cup.

"When the tornado passed, there you were, rising up out of the lake looking like you did—full of mud and seaweed—then you giving us what for, well, you got our attention." He winced lowering his gaze as he seemed to gather strength to continue.

"All last night, I couldn't stop thinking about what happened and about the things you were yelling, so I decided to head out for a bike ride to shake those thoughts. Before I left, I felt something inside me saying, 'Put a helmet on.' It was so strong—and I haven't worn a helmet in over thirty years—but I did."

The others nodded in silent agreement.

"No sooner was I down the road, than three deer ran out in front of me. I had to put the bike down in a slide, then jump off before it ran into a guardrail." He turned his bloodshot eyes to Adam. "Doc says if I hadn't put that helmet on, I would have cracked my head open like a melon."

One of The Nine picked up Grizzly's helmet and showed the hit marks.

"Remember when you said our sins are piled in front of us?"

"Yes, very well." Adam's blood quickened as he recalled his hot-tempered speech.

"After I'd hit my head, the next thing I knew, the paramedics were carrying me to the ambulance. And in front of me was a man telling me I was on my way to the hospital and not to worry, he'd get my bike home."

Grizzly stopped there, holding back a tear with a tightening throat before he could go on. "This man was someone we, as a group, had been pretty cruel to the other day. I couldn't get it. He was being kind to me, telling me not to worry, acting like we had never done nothin' to him, his wife, or one of their dogs." He adjusted his sheets as if they were bothering him.

"Adam, we've never heard of any of that stuff you were talking about yesterday, but with everything that's happened, well, we decided we need to know more."

Pa took over and told The Nine about John 3:16 and how to ask Christ into their lives, including praying a sinner's prayer with them.

Getting back in the van, Pa sat with his hands clasped on the steering wheel. Then he spoke up, "We will be moving here."

And, as Pa started the engine, Adam wept.

But this wasn't finished yet.

On the way home, Pa pulled into Mr. Tarsh's yard, finding him returning from walking his two dogs.

"Good evening, folks. Come on in."

Adam followed him inside, *dropping* to one knee to greet the dogs while the gentleman introduced them to Emily, his wife. Then Pa let them know they were returning from Grace Hospital where they'd seen Grizzly.

"How is he doing?" Mr. Tarsh braced one hand on the counter, his face soft with concern as if the cruel event never happened.

"First, I have to ask, was it you who helped him on the road last night?"

"Yes."

"And from what we hear, you went out of your way to be nice to him."

Emily walked over to her husband and stood beside him. With her arms around his waist, she rested her head against his shoulder, and then Nathan shared what had transpired when they were heading home from their Thursday night study group. The topic had been on forgiving those who had done them wrong, heartbreaking wrong.

"Jon, this could only have been planned by God because we were following a study book we had been into for a good month now. The Scripture was on loving your enemy. Oh, we know we are to heap coals of kindness, but the writer gave an explanation of, 'If someone killed your loved one or a beloved dog, could you turn the other cheek and offer that person Christ?' I almost walked out then, but somehow, I stayed and listened to the end. The teaching was simple. 'If you can't forgive, ask the heavenly Father to help you, and He will make the way."

Mr. Tarsh's face went serious as he took a chair at the table, then hand-gestured for his guest to sit also. Folding his hands as if in prayer, he continued.

"The other night as we were on our way home, driving down Old Broken Hill Road, we came upon someone laying right on the road. We saw what was a bloody heap." He took a deep breath, ending with a sigh. "We recognized whose motorcycle it was." He closed his eyes, then laid his head in his hands, shoveling his fingers through his hair as he shared the next part.

"Jon, when we got out of that car, we stood, staring at him. In the back of both our minds, we realized we'd been given the chance to do what we learned a little earlier. But God gives you a good counselor in a godly wife. My sweet Emily said, 'You stay with him. I'll get help.' " Mr. Tarsh opened his eyes. "When she left, I thought, 'If I had a frying pan…' But then, I ended up having to tell God I didn't have the strength to forgive him, and I asked the Good Lord, 'Please, help me!' Without feeling like it, I did what was right. When the paramedics came, I was starting to feel better inside, just from doing what was right."

Adam saddened, but understood, seeing it not as man's failed bits and pieces, but as God's whole perfect work.

Mr. and Mrs. Tarsh then shared their plans to take over caring for The Nine—everything from making them soup, to helping them know Christ and His love.

CHAPTER 15

UNLOCKING THE HIDDEN CODE WITHIN

Moving down to the Tipperville was in one way hard. To their dismay, they had to leave behind their oldest three sons and their wives. The oldest, Dan, a doctor, couldn't leave his patients till someone was able to fill in. The next two sons were torn between the connecting families. They wanted to stay behind and farm for Dan and Kally while they worked. They promised to come as soon as God opened their doors. The aunts and uncles on both sides came to the same conclusion: they would visit first and then make up their minds.

To Ma and Pa's comfort, the new home would now consist of the last three of their married daughters and their husbands. Three close male cousins just a little older than Adam came along as well. They were looking for adventure. Figuring if they went, their parents would soon follow.

God had guided the Stands there and proved it as the Sutton farm worked out well. With more rooms than they could use, they made extra bedrooms for the expanded family. Marlene reported to Jon every night about how much she loved the place, and she hoped the rest of the family would come soon.

Grandma Clip and Grandma Stands settled right in also. This new team, nicknamed "the girls," involved itself in all sorts of projects, and the new church was just the place for them. Program Fix It, In The Name Of Jesus was their doing.

In the five years since their move, Ma lost her only brother to cancer. He'd been the father of Shad, one of the cousins who'd moved down with them. The young man brought his mother to a small cottage built next to the Stands for extra family. Eventually, she moved to the main house, preferring not to be by herself, exchanging the cottage with the single young men.

During the past two years, Tipperville enacted a new ordinance for all in and around town. Everyone who was able now had to volunteer in one or more of the community departments—fire department, fueling storage and stations, policing, electric, fresh water, roads, communication, and of course, sanitation. The next town over housed Grace Hospital, which ran the only electrical plant and turbine windmill to supply the area's needs. But Mayor Ned, acting president, called all the shots. Under his authority, the younger people would receive training to take over all the jobs.

Mayor Ned hand chose four of the young Stands men, claiming he found them all to be wise and quick to learn. Shad was to be the head of the fire department. Adam liked the road department; Mac, the electrical; Abe, fuel and compound storage. All four volunteered at least twenty-five hours a week. First, because they liked it, and second, because they had extra hands on the farm. The mayor also noted that, since they were in one household, the four were able to help each other in emergencies.

"Tonight's town meeting is going to be tough for everyone," Mac remarked as he skimmed paperwork he'd brought home from work.

"How's that?" Abe paused in drying the supper dishes.

Mac leaned his chair back on two legs. "The coal miners are starting to shut down. They don't want to be underground anymore, and gas is getting harder to get. Then there are the road conditions. They have to drive with an armed guard because of hijacking."

Adam tugged on a clean shirt, tossing the dirty one on Mac's head. "We'd better head on over. Even with my department, there's going to be a lot to discuss tonight."

He ducked as Mac tossed the dirty shirt back at him hard. "I have a hard time with the mayor. You know what he did this morning? He felt God had been telling him that *my* inner self was a mess and I needed clear crystals."

Rolling his eyes, Adam waddled his head. "Get this—he was trying to give me some of those crystals to wear for my own good." He threw his hand up in a stopping stance. "I told him I was a Christian and I don't accept any of that stuff is from God. He told me he is a Christian, too, and the crystals come from God's earth. He learned God made them with special powers for us to use."

"Whoa, yeah," Abe added. "I picked up on things he had all around his office and thought they looked pretty strange. I figured he was into something."

An hour later, they entered the old high school auditorium. Those who were important had tables and chairs on stage, and the rest sat at their favorite unassigned seats. The Stands men took their places on stage. Just about everyone who lived in or around town attended now. For those who couldn't attend, someone would visit afterward to keep them informed about the constant changes. The old small-town meeting had changed again.

Everything was straightforward until the Stands men were to report on their respective departments.

Mayor Ned tapped the paper before him and leaned toward the Stands. "Mac, next on the agenda is your report on the electrical progress."

"Yes, sir." Mac nodded his head, then shook it as he spoke. "But today's report is not going to be a good one."

A general rustling moved through the crowd as they directed their attention to Mac.

Adam leaned back and folded his arms. At least, Mac seemed to absorb the scowls well.

"There will have to be more blackouts scheduled for our area, starting next week." As gasps and whispers of "oh no" resounded, Mac lifted tired eyes to the crowd. "The problems are several. The power station is weakening. Many parts are out of date. Not enough workers. With things from the disappearing factories and safety issues, it is not enough. The larger boilers are already ten years out of date. They were built for forty."

Adam scanned his friends and neighbors. A sort of denial, coupled with acceptance of the inevitable, set their expression. Everyone knew this would come, but their hearts feared to face it.

The weight in his heart lifted as his gaze stopped at Silvia Johnston, the pretty gal keeping the meeting's minutes. Every once in a while, she stilled her pen while Mac caught her eye, saying much in a single glance. He'd have to rib him later.

Mac shook his head, the intensity returning his brow to a grim set. "Grace Hospital is the number-one priority on the gridline. We cannot let anything compromise its power. With the turbine windmill working, it may be okay for about five more years. Three nursing homes are also on the north grid. Paul Morris prepared for these twenty-five years ago, with plans of the decreasing electricity use."

Mac passed Adam, along with his cousins, papers to hand out to everyone. But Mac conveniently handed one to Silvia. As he moved through the crowd, Adam glanced over his shoulder. The petite woman scanned the papers and then gazed at Mac as if it was her duty to watch him. Yep. He'd have to increase his teasing before he lost Mac completely.

"Don't I get one?" a high-pitched voice demanded.

"Oh!" Adam spun back to the tweed-suited man before him. "So sorry, sir. I was… distracted."

"So I saw. Pretty girl." The elderly man winked, and heat tingled up Adam's neck. He hurried on along the line, unable to explain *he* wasn't the one making eyes at Silvia.

As everyone was reading what they could, Mac continued. "If you look at these sheets, you'll see where I have laid out the electrical grids and graphed the power outages for each area, day, and time. I've included a list of legal and illegal equipment. Remember one light on in a house at any given time. Please. You may use a washer, but no dryer. No electrical clocks, heaters—well, I'm not going over this whole list since most of it you already know. What you don't know is, as of now, anyone using more than allotted will be shut off. The floor will be open for questions." He stepped back and sat down with a tenacious tilt to his chin. The one he used when Adam or Shad tried to argue some game's rules.

Hanna Kline raised a knobby hand. In her sixties, the delicate woman had survived the car accident that took her husband. The list quivered in her left hand, her arthritic fingers seeming to struggle to clutch it. "I need a mixer for my hands for cooking, but it's on the list."

"Yes, Mrs. Kline. If you, or anyone else, have any handicaps, we can make adjustments. But you may want to consider starting a group to work together for cooking and chores."

The people studied the papers and whispered back and forth. Some pinched their lips tight, their scowls deepening. One older gentleman twitched his hand up and then planted it firmly in his lap. Like the others, he wanted to argue but knew he couldn't—they were all living on gifted time. With what they heard from others passing through, they took what was still available and tried to adjust.

"Now, the mine is looking for workers, and there are perks to living next to the electrical plant. But they also have their limits. If you can farm, my advice is farm. People have lived without electricity for centuries, but they can't live without food."

Next, Abe addressed the fuel storage. He gave a full report of kerosene and gas amounts in storage. His department also had problems with thieves.

Adam's report added that things were changing because he hadn't seen any traffic from the Raleigh area in about a week.

When he'd finished, Silvia spoke up. "Mayor, maybe we should send Adam or someone out to check the roads in a certain radius. He does need to know the road conditions. Who knows if there is a bridge out? And, I was thinking, we could see if someone could bring back some needed supplies, like peddlers in the olden days."

"I have been thinking about checking out what *is* going on out there," Adam admitted with a quickening in his chest as he spoke, "and seeing what roads are safe, kept up. It has gotten a lot quieter lately, other than Graceville."

Everyone agreed he should go, and Adam's heart to travel loved the idea. They concluded the meeting with other reports and one old lady telling Adam she needed a new mattress for her back, so he should keep an eye out for a good one. As they passed the mayor's desk, they saw three crystals in the shape of pyramids. He looked at the others knowingly.

In the predawn hour came the call: a fire. The Stands men hurried from the warmth of their beds. The call came in for the Millers' barn, five miles down the road. When they arrived, the glow from the fire lit up the barn area from the circling darkness. A smaller barn had already been eaten up by flames, and those flames were reaching over and licking up the walls of the main large one. The Millers and friends were scrambling to pull equipment and stock further away.

Shad, being in charge, was fast on his feet in every way, leading those helping while sizing up the fight. Even the mayor showed up to help as his civic duty. But, being a man who was usually in charge, Mayor Ned started to interfere with Shad's job. Knowing the fire would spread to the house if they were not careful in what they do, Shad tried to keep the mayor busy, so he could concentrate on his job and sent him to check on how many volunteers they had working now.

But the terrifying news came back that two men were missing. Shad and Abe donned their gas masks, and when Mac heard, he insisted on gearing up to join them.

The three marched to the barn when the mayor ran up alongside them, trying to hand each of them rocks, yelling out, "Here, carry these. They will protect you!"

"No thanks, mayor!" Shad yelled back as he pushed the mayor's hand away. "God Jehovah sent His Son to be the one we will rely on. No matter the outcome."

"Don't be stupid! These rocks are the power of protection. Take them."

"Mayor, if we take them, we will die!"

As the three stormed off, Shad yelled to Adam, "Keep the hoses continually going right where we enter. We'll need a way out."

The smoked rolled, heat intense, as the three walked on into danger. The roof above in that one split second collapsed. Tongues of lapping flames became the new door to the opening. Holding his breath—not from the smoke—Adam kept his hose focused on the doorway, but it never dampened this fire's intensity. Heat scorched his face. Smoke burned his eyes as he squinted into the flames, straining to see if even one of his cousins would run out.

The mayor grabbed the fire truck's bucket and rose it up in over the roof opening, to see if he could help anyone then. When the bucket reached the right height, the mayor jerked sideways.

"What do you see, Ned?" Old Charlie shouted for Mayor Ned was shaking.

Wouldn't he answer? Adam focused the water on the doorway, his ears on the mayor.

"Sir?" *Say something, Mr. Mayor!*

"I… I see…" He held his hand before his face as if to shield it. Then shook his head and choked out more words. "I see four men walking around below, right in the center of this intense fiery furnace. Lower me! It's too hot here."

As the bucket touched down, the two presumed missing men came back from tending the Millers' stock.

Adam's shoulders and his arms vibrated from the water's force. Still, he kept it trained on the entrance. Beside him, Mayor Ned squinted into the opaque fire, then at the rocks still clutched in his hand. Throwing them down, he called to the men to come out, and at that moment, they did. However, there were three, not four.

As their neighbors gawked, the three walked out as if nothing were wrong. Mayor Ned ran to them, touching them in a greeting, turning their arms and hands to display no hot spots or ash. "I'm sorry!" His eyes were crunched in a sorrowful look. "You are right about God. He needs no stones that He created to do what He is capable of doing Himself. I will deal with those who have been teaching me otherwise."

Tears gleamed in the mayor's eyes when Shad approached. "I felt Him, you know, mayor. Christ, I felt as if He were walking with us in the fire."

"I saw Him—He *was* walking around with you." The mayor's voice quavered. "I had them lift me up in the fire truck's bucket to see if there was any hope." He gazed at Shad with glazed eyes. "There was a fourth man with you, walking along with you. I saw Him. It was Christ Jesus Himself."

The men finished their jobs and headed to the station to prepare their equipment for the next moment's notice.

Later that morning, they sat at the kitchen table, having coffee and talking about the Millers' barn when a knock jostled the door. Too tired to move, Adam merely gazed up at the door. With a short curtain over the lower half window, he could only see the tops of heads. Many heads. He shoved back his chair and reached for the handle. As he opened it, a rush of familiar voices surrounded him. Hands slapped his back. Arms hugged his neck. The rest of the Stands family had finally come.

His three oldest siblings, their spouses tagging behind, and twenty extended family members flowed into the Stands' kitchen, including one unfamiliar little old lady.

"I know you said to come, Dad." Dan smiled. "But we didn't think you'd mind." He pointed over his shoulder with his thumb at the tired group.

Now the Stands had something to do, and they took on the task with a prayer of thanks.

CHAPTER 16

CAN A MAN BE LOVED SO MUCH?

Adam spent the next days mapping out places he should check. His brothers informed him about the changes they'd had to go through to get there, including the difficulty getting gas. They had waited five days for gas at one government station, thinking they were never going to get anywhere. People had piled up in lines unable to move on. Huge boulders blocked a road in the west. The detour not only took hours longer but also seemed worse to drive over than the original avalanche.

The night before Adam left, Robby, his second older brother, wandered into his room. "Can you take someone with you? It's pretty strange out there in some areas. How about if I come along?"

"Thanks, but no thanks. One can maneuver around easier than two. And Mom would kill me if you left, now that she's you got here."

To Adam's surprise, the mayor gave him an L-van to drive. The L-car, vans, and trucks were conveniently created the year God had announced His plan. Without computers or any extras to power anything, they would be considerably slower, but easier to repair, and with updated ingenuity, they would get 100 miles to the gallon. He packed tools, a sleeping bag, a change of clothes, an emergency kit, extra fuel, and food with no problem.

Winds and rain darkened the morning, but they did not dampen his traveling heart. As the L-van eased along, he talked to God, praising Him for this chance.

Roads showed tremendous needs of repair. Horses and L-cars were easier on the roads, but the cracks kept widening. When plants took seed, the roots expanded the cracks to meet their need.

Men and women from all around moved into houses they never would have been able to afford before. Someone's abandoned luxury retirement became a temptation to those who'd never had it so nice. But what good was a fancy home on a cliff with a great view when they wouldn't be able to feed themselves?

Even though it had been happening for years, it was weird to see a motor home stranded at the roadside due to lacking gas or parts. Cars, trucks, even buses were also just pushed aside.

Just twenty-five years ago, man had it all. But all this shows me I am on the edge of the next change. Whatever it is.

Every once in a while, he'd check some of the abandoned cars, RVs, or trucks. They looked like some large animal had up and died. Most had been stripped for parts.

One gruesome one contained gross-smelling decomposing bodies. They were fly festering and oozing. Not being able to bury these people, he tied in branches into a shape of a cross and placed it on the hood.

Before he left the area, he checked his map, his finger tracing the road he was on to a large bridge up ahead.

A quarter of an hour later, he came to a stop before the bridge. The click of his door opening echoed in the empty atmosphere. The lonely sound somehow giving him the shivers, he got out and gazed over a gap in the middle of the bridge. The bridge rose about two hundred feet up and spanned maybe three hundred feet. No one had put up a warning sign. How many people had or could plunge to their deaths without it?

Dizzied by the height, he knelt on the ravine's gravel ledge. At the bottom, a large, burned-out area blackened the land by the river. In it, a semi truck had burned up on impact, scorching about seventy feet around it. Crumbled piles of the fallen concrete gave the appearance of gravestones marking the area.

It took him the rest of the day to block every inch of his side off with logs and branches. Convinced it would do the job, he added foil from his van, wrapping it around several branches to reflect headlights approaching in the night.

With dusk thickening, mist rose from the river below, the eerily beautiful wisps warning of the dangers of night travel. So he fixed up a fire, brought over more dried wood, made his bed in the van, and proceeded to toast bread and cheese for himself. He garnished his meal with home-dried beef jerky and ate some cookies his sisters gave him and a slice from one of two pies Ma sent along. *Wow, I should go away more often!* He chuckled and leaned back on his hands, peering into the deepening twilight.

As the dark claimed its time to be, Adam walked over to view the downed bridge. Lights marked homes he never would have known were there. Seven twinkled from the bridge's left view, and one winked at him far up the other side.

How vast and beautiful was this world, but how alone he was becoming in it. Shaking his head, he went back and sat on a log by the crackling fire, poking at it here and there. *Too bad I never learned to play a guitar or a harmonica. It sure would have been cool to be able to sit by a fire and roll out some tunes.* Finding not too much else to do in the dark, he headed for bed.

The early morning sun was busy trying to creep into the van while Adam stirred a little here and a little there. Being young, he was still able to sleep anywhere. Even though it wasn't his in own bed, he was comfortable.

Not wanting to get up yet, he eyed the thin metal sides, thinking about the day ahead, when something hit the van with a loud thump and dented it inside. The van started to rock from one side to the other, and as whatever it was pummeled it, it caved in spots here and there. Reaching around to his side where he'd placed his handgun the night before, he scrambled toward the front. Then jolted, freezing in place.

Five lions lurked outside, and two were trying to get in.

No way could I kill even one with such a small caliber. He rammed his hand on the car horn to scare them. It only startled them for a moment. Grabbing for his keys in his pocket, he dropped them.

As he stooped to recover them, he faced one lioness about forty feet away—looking directly at him. They locked eyes, the golden orbs strangely hypnotic.

The lion crouched, shoulders bunching, hind rising. If it broke into a run, it would bust through the window. He scooped up the keys, hands shaking as he selected the silver one. It slipped in his sweating fingers, jamming against the ignition, and then bounced to the floorboard, landing behind the gas pedal.

The lioness charged, just a blur of tawny color. Then, mouth wide open, she slobbered the glass. A giant paw scratched marks into the windshield, the sound cringing through him.

He slid to the passenger seat, gun in hand, and started to roll down the window.

Feeling as if he were in one of those dreams where he worked or ran in slow motion, he put his gun through the window and fired—*boom, boom, boom, boom, boom, boom!*

The lions scattered. But with the area thick with brush, he couldn't trust they were gone. His heart slammed his ribs, beating almost out of his chest as he groped for the keys and jammed them into the ignition. When he finally started the van, he drove to where he left his things the night before, and leaning out the window, yet keeping watch, he scooped them up. Remembering their speed, he was taking no chances. When he left, he looked back. The male had returned and was standing in the road, watching him drive away.

All morning long, he kept replaying it in his mind. Were they pets set loose or from some zoo? He shuddered as he remembered being outside the day and night before. They would kill, and he could do nothing. There were enough of them to be called a pride.

Two days of talking to people, and rating towns, roads, and businesses kept him busy. He spread word of the lions. Making changes on his road map, he traveled south, then east, then north. He was approaching the final city, the one closed off by the downed bridge.

As he came in from the farming side, the fields enveloped him in colors of soon-to-be harvest, though he could see where they'd fade to the city again. But out in a field, he saw something. Or was it someone? It was a man… yes, a man. About a hundred feet away, the man was bent over as if grazing with donkeys. The strange man's long gray hair blew in the wind like plumes of an exotic bird.

When Adam slowed to a stop, the man stood, fixing his eyes on Adam. With fingers curved with nails so long they had the appearance of talons, he lifted his hand and pointed to Adam. The wild man resumed his stooped position again, hunched over, even though he was a man. Dirt caked his face, but his body glistened from the morning dew.

The animal like man tilted his head like a dog looking at his master and trying to understand what was being said. He tipped it back and forth, squinting at Adam, and then smiled as if he somehow knew him. The strange man then faced the heavens and started saying something. He peered back at Adam, and with a raise of one hand, he waved as if biding a dear friend goodbye. He then remained on two feet while walking away.

Baffled, Adam drove on.

After driving another five miles to this cutoff city, he needed to pull over to study it. He saw no one moving around. *It must be abandoned. So then why is there only one road closed?*

Shattered glass cast prisms below a few damaged storefronts. Overgrown or dried-out shrubs lost their decorative effect and tangled with downed wires, some catching the trash that always seemed to follow wherever man had been.

Adam's high alert eased as the warm sun and chirping birds of this quiet city let him move in and around it in peace. Until one storefront caught his interest—Mattress City. He got out to peek in the window and test the door. It opened with ease to an empty floor with only a couple of desks and filing cabinets hugging a corner. Sale signs lay in the dust, reminding him of days gone by. One last peek in the back room. And there it lay like a golden fleece, a mattress, wrapped up tightly in plastic, leaning on its side as if waiting in the silence for someone, anyone.

Bold black letters on the note taped to the foamy twin mattress promised, "You can have it."

Remembering the older woman at the town meeting, Adam chuckled. "She must be praying." He tucked the note in his pocket and locked onto his new traveling companion. "Now, to get you into the van."

The wobbly mattress flopped over his shoulder, sandwiching him beneath it. He bumped into the doorway and set it down, rubbing his chin as he considered how to angle it through without dragging it on the dirty floor or scraping it on the sidewalk outside.

A deep voice behind him said, "Can I give you a hand?"

Adam turned to a guy about his age. "Sorry, is this yours?"

"Nope. Sorry, is that yours?" The guy pointed over at Adam's van being plundered by a group of men and women helping themselves to his possessions inside.

Adam's eyes grew wide, and his breath stopped for a second. "Hey, stop!" He sprinted toward the door. "That's my van!"

"Too late, man." The stranger laid a cautioning hand on Adam's arm. "Stay here, and I'll see what I can do."

Then he strode over and talked to the group. When he returned, he shrugged. "You lost all your food, including two pies, but they agreed to leave the rest."

A lanky tall man held Adam's last bag of homemade cookies high into the air while doing a victory dance.

"Thanks. I owe you, I guess." Adam tried to calm his racing heart. They hadn't taken it all. He'd been blessed. He cast a rueful smile toward this guy, who ambled over to put down a guitar, his cowboy boots clomping on the cement floor.

"I'm Adam Stands, and I'm on the road department over in Tipperville. We were wondering why we hadn't seen anyone from this area of late, so I've been out scouting."

"I'm called King." Ambling closer, King extended a hand to shake. A friendly smile curved his kind face. "You see that group of people? They follow me wherever I go. If I said jump, while they were in midair, they'd ask how high."

"Wow. How come?"

King strolled over to the window and gazed at those gathered. They sat around talking. Every once in a while, they looked for him. "Because I can sing, and I'm good—really, really good—at it." His voice was not only deep but slow.

"They follow you because you can sing?"

"Yep, and I told you, I'm really, really good." He turned to Adam. "Let's load you up, and then I'll show you." He went over to the mattress and helped Adam lift it. As soon as they started out the door, his followers ran up and took over.

"Hey, King, you could hurt yourself or your hand." A lanky but muscular man winked, scooped the mattress up with one hand, and slung it over his shoulder. "Let me get that."

King backed away, smiling.

One woman in baggy jeans and graying black straggly hair ran up to Adam and growled low to him, "You never make the King do *anything*. He could get hurt, and if he did…" She paused to lean in, lowering her head till he only could see her dark warning eyes. "We would kill you."

Adam gawked. *She meant it. I'm out of here!*

After they loaded the mattress, King called out, "Now, Adam, come on over. I'll treat you to a song."

Adam lifted his hand and shook his head, but a man standing next to him gripped his arm.

Hot breath seethed into Adam's ear. "You *do not* insult the King. If the King wants to perform for you, you'd best be thankful and accept."

"Oh, sorry." Adam stumbled along, half-dragged to where he was to sit as the rest of the crowd gathered, smiling.

"Now, I'm dedicating this song to my new friend, Adam." While King warmed up his guitar, men next to Adam warned him to applaud real loud in thanks as he would not want to offend their King. *Their King?* Adam thought. Then their King began to play.

The man's voice rose and fell in swooping momentum, his fingers danced in one with the guitar strings, delivering such coaxing sounds. Sounds Adam had never heard come from any person he knew who could sing. Others melted in with complementary instruments that appeared from somewhere. Women swayed and danced. King had a hold on all of them with just his voice. Fifteen minutes later, he stopped, and they whined as if they were dogs that had the gifted bones and then had them taken away.

One guy next to Adam clapped him on the back, nearly slamming him forward in his exuberance. "Thanks, man! The King hadn't wanted to sing for over a week. That was a real treat!"

King strolled over and invited Adam to stay for dinner and to spend the night. The group in earshot glared at Adam, their eyes warning him not to decline. Some even walked toward him as a threat. After Adam took the hint, he was directed to a hotel, the commandeered home of these people. Three men rode along with him so he couldn't take off, telling King they were going to give him a hand.

The King never knew.

At the hotel, they gave Adam a room on the fifth floor, taking him up by stairs, claiming the elevator no longer ran, and then waking him down a hallway only lit by doors left open on both sides so window light could spill in.

"Those on the right side face the indoor pool court, but they have little light from the overhead skylights. We use these. Large outside windows face southwest, for more light. The water comes from the roof, so use it only when necessary."

The room offered only a bed and a dresser.

One of the men thrust out a hand and said, "Hand them over!"

"What?"

"The keys to your van!" a beefy man growled, looming closer, the studs on his leather vest clicking. His voice seemed to fill the room and echo in Adam's head. "You go nowhere. If you make our King happy, we'll treat you fine, but if you upset him, well, we don't care what happens to you."

Adam handed them the van keys, and they left, leaving the door wide open. He stood unmoving, facing his one window. Then he turned, and he shut *his* door.

An hour later, Adam's door slammed open. Instantly, he prepared himself for a confrontation by jumping off his bed. But to his surprise, three rough-looking tattooed women brazenly walked into his personal space.

One stepped even closer. "Dinner will be served outside, and the King is expecting you. Now!" She wasn't asking. She was commanding.

Then her face changed to excitement, including her words. "Hey, the rumor is that you put the King in a good mood, so the King will probably be playing for us tonight."

As quick as she finished, her face changed back to squinting eyes with an unspoken growl. "Mr. Adam, I shall give you a warning. Whatever you do, *don't* put him in a bad mood."

With that, they started to lead him back down the dark hallway when their countenance changed again. They were like excited teen girls and talking amongst themselves.

Adam followed as they channeled him to the stairs he came up. Once they got to the lobby, he was pushed with a firm hand through another door by old unstable elevators. That door brought them into a short dark hall with two more turns until they faced side-by-side swinging doors propped open like a wide mouth of a lion. In there, they made their way across what used to be the pool court to doors to an outside patio. A beautiful dinner patio waited, equipped with tables, chairs, and a stage built with fake rocks all around. Even the overgrowth added to its tranquil beauty.

No sooner was Adam seated than they offered him some sort of stew that looked almost gooey, but once the spoon passed his lips, he knew there'd be nothing left on his plate. As he ate, he observed the surrounding talk. None of it was of any value, and these folk could not say a sentence without decorating it with a bouquet of swear words. So he tuned them out and talked to God, asking Him to show him a way out. He never heard King address him.

Someone kicked hard on the side of his chair. One of the men who'd escorted him earlier scowled at him with an even tougher-looking woman by his side.

Their backs were to King, who sat on the steps of the stage, warming up his guitar with some other musicians. In a gruff, low voice so the King couldn't hear, he swore at Adam and told him not to mess up the King's mood or he would pay.

"Now, smile at him and act glad—no, be excited—to hear him play for you."

Adam pivoted to King, oblivious to what was going on. He yelled out a greeting and waved. King waved, then rose, and pranced up the rest of the way on the stage.

The people scurried like ants to a dropped cookie. Sitting down, they didn't take their gazes off him.

Then King put on a show that even had Adam's toes tapping. Later, drenched with sweat from an all-out performance, he strolled over and sat by Adam. His people clapped him on the back. Women kissed him. All were in smiles, just for the King, and King looked humbly back at them.

"So, Adam, what did ya think?"

"You were right. You're good—really, really good. And I want to thank you for this great show. When I leave tomorrow, I'll never forget it."

"Leave? No way, friend, you can't." King leaned back in his chair and dabbed his forehead with a cloth. "You're not that into it, are you?"

Adam was about to answer when King got up. "Come on." Some men shoved their chairs back to rise, but King waved at them to sit back. "Hey, guys, give me a break. I'll see you all later."

The men gave Adam a warning look as King led him to the empty indoor pool court. Inside, he grabbed a reclining chair and offered one to Adam. King lit five candles, and then they talked for hours. King said he found Adam to be honest and interesting. As Adam relaxed more, they talked, and each discovered a friend. Adam not only discussed his family but also his faith, and King listened, saying he was taking away a lot to think about.

Only darkness lined the corridor as Adam headed back to his room where his guards joined him. "What were you and the King talking about?"

"About the God who is in my life."

"God? So you're one of those. Don't talk no God to the King. We like him just the way he is." They cussed him and warned him again not to try to leave, then left.

The next morning, Adam was still sleeping when a bold knock hit the door.

"Get up! The King will be heading for breakfast soon, and he wants you to join him."

Adam settled deeper into the bed and quilt, stretching out his protesting muscles as every bit of him cried out to turn over and ignore their summons. It had taken him a while to fall asleep last night. His mind kept rolling all night, thinking about everything. He sighed and tossed aside the warm quilt, feet hitting the floor to follow his instructions.

Outside, King had already started eating. Pancakes, syrup, fruits, and eggs spread across the table before him. Where they had gotten them, who knew? King not only was treated like a king, but he ate like one, too.

At breakfast, they continue their conversation from the night before. As the conversation slowed, Adam slid in, "Sorry to say, King, but I have to be going."

"Man, couldn't you stick around, teach me and the rest?" King pointed to the others with his butter knife.

"Nope. I have got to go. I have people counting on me, and it wouldn't be right. I have a Bible in my van I can leave you, and God will take care of the rest. Could you get your friends to get the keys for my van?"

"Why do they have the keys?"

"Oh, I suppose they were keeping an eye on it for me. I hate to leave, but one thing I do know is God always shows Himself to those who seek Him."

"Sure, and I'll hunt around for a Bible and ask that God of yours to teach me."

Adam lightly laughed. "And you could even write and sing to God some of them special songs of yours, once you get to know Him."

When Adam retrieved his keys, he shook hands with King and received a hug with a slap on the back. As he turned to enter the pool court, people start to scream. Spinning around, he jumped—for a pride of lions was walking across the stage. Man's enemy had crossed the river and were hunting man again as their desired food.

People ran, pushing each other out of the way. Adam darted inside the indoor pool court. Twisting his head back, he cringed.

The same huge male lion from the fallen bridge area locked eyes with him once again. Without hesitation, it broke into a headlong run straight for him.

He fumbled and slipped trying to pull shut the door. The rest of the pride now joined the male, till all were only fifteen feet away and focused on him. But the door wouldn't close. Adam continued to back in, circling around the empty pool's far side.

The lions, who had now slowed to a walk, were investigating the entrance as they targeted him, roaring with each step. Then the reluctant door closed with all inside.

The morning light filtered through the skylight outlining each lion's face. They stood, unmoving, sizing up their trapped meal. Then each lions' demeanor changed.

Ears laid back, their eyes looked around as they started to pace as though seeking a way out.

That's when the floor began to rumble. The walls vibrated like a dog shaking off water. Adam thrust his hands out to brace himself. Ceiling tiles crackled loose and began to fall. He leaped into the empty pool and ran to the deepest side, hugging the wall. The sounds erupted as this quake disturbed the ground. It roared as if it were a giant lion about to devour them. Crashing and cracking accompanied each and every movement.

Then it slowed. Then stopped. Dust rolled in the air, choking Adam and what light there was.

When King had seen the lions, he'd taken off for the kitchen, following the others. He'd thought Adam was right behind him. Only, when he looked back, he gasped, seeing Adam racing toward the pool court with the lions darting after as they locked onto their prey.

One of the other men ran up to the pool's door closing the lions and Adam inside. King ran to help his new friend. But the ground began to rumble. He had to stop, bracing his steps until, in disbelief, he realized what it was.

The large overhang above the pool entrance collapsed, blocking the entrance with heavy concrete and metal debris. Windows blew apart, parts of the building crumbled off, and people screamed. When the moving ground stilled, King's heart was beating faster and harder than during any performance he'd ever given.

People called to each other, asking what had happened and checking on those who might have been hurt.

King stood, looking at the blocked door, then yelled for his men to help him get Adam out.

"It's too late," someone shouted. "He's trapped with the lions, and they're probably eating him right now."

"No! We're going in to help him." Running into the side entrance, he called, "Come on."

They followed him in a side off the kitchen, avoiding things that had crashed. Leaping over turned debris, they wound through the halls into the main lobby. Coughing from the rising dust, they covered their noses and mouths with their shirts. At the hallway to enter the pool court, King stilled. The walls and the ceiling had broken away, blocking their only path.

He thought for a second, trying to respond like a great leader, and then waved over to the stairs leading up. "Come on. Up there!"

The first floor was blocked, and the second was blocked. But the third floor was clear. King led them to a balcony off one room facing the pool court. Testing it, he leaned out and cried into the roiling dust, "Adam, please tell me your God saved you from all this!"

"Well, King," a response wavered from down below, "I'm fine, but, boy, am I glad to hear your voice. The lions haven't touched me. It seems my God *is* keeping me safe, and I'm glad to hear He has done the same for you. Can you get me out?"

"You just hang on, and I'll send down a rope."

They tied together the curtains from the other rooms, taking more time than King could bear as lions stalked all around Adam. They even brushed against him at times. When his men lowered the rope, Adam made it into a harness so they were able to lift him to safety. The lions just paced.

"I would have never believed it if I hadn't seen it with my own eyes!" King hugged Adam with praises of his own going out to his new God.

On the next balcony over stood the three self-appointed watchmen. One cursed and yelled over. "Don't be fooled, King! Those lions didn't touch him because they were still upset from the quake. There ain't no God!"

In that instant, the floors began to shake again. An aftershock rumbled to those men's balcony. The cement broke loose, sliding them down. Even before they hit the ground, they belonged to the lions.

CHAPTER 17

AND THEN THE LIGHTS FLICKERED

Adam returned home to give a full report. Because of his shared stories, the family began praying for King and his fans. Daily chores, including tending births of new stock or planting for the next season, filled the following spring months. All those who moved down with Dan and his wife were blessed with land connecting one to another to help each other in raising and growing food.

One scary incident occurred in town when strangers came… thieves. It ended with an unavoidable shootout. Those caught in the act didn't want to surrender, forcing the end of losing their lives. Those involved had to let time, with God's help, heal them from the trauma.

Tipperville's citizens never gave up trying to be wise about their future and locating problems they could fix. They completed projects such as tearing down rotting barns and replacing them with a barn raising.

During the next years, Adam and his family faced the loss of good friends, young and old. But it never decreased the number of people around. People flowed from the north, filling gaps. And, good gracious, if someone was to marry, the whole town got involved in the fun, ready to dance as they had back when Mac and Silvia wed.

The work was hard, but good. The Stands were leaders in showing others how to work together. Helping their fellow men in patience and kindness, they left a trail of the Good Lord. If a field had to be cleared of rocks, there were more than enough hands to complete the work quickly, and the clever women always had places for the rocks to go like an outside cookstove to save their homes from the unbearable summer heat.

People also learned to be ready with hugs for their neighbors any time they were needed.

Hope was one of those intangible things that could be lost during the changing times. But it could be found in plenty of ways, in places one would never think.

Five years from Adam's venture at this time faded to a memory. Then the dreaded change of life as they knew it happened as the Stands sat for their evening meal. The long-dreaded signal—the lights flickered ten times on then off. The frightening code saying it was ending. Electricity. They sat in silence. No one moved for a while, knowing the great ruler would never breathe again.

Then Marlene got up, went to the oil lamps on the side hutch, lit the lanterns, and laughed. "I wondered when that was going to happen."

Hospitals, factories, and government service areas were the only places still serviced with electricity, and they only existed on its last few breaths. Now, not even the nursing homes were granted electricity, resulting in many deaths that night and in the following days as the machines on which the lingering bodies relied ceased to function. The only way anyone could speak up was to ask God for grace or strength. This new level of man hoped they had mastered enough of the old ways, the ways before electricity. Electrical things had no value and were tossed aside.

As she was clearing the table, she stopped and gasped. "Mrs. Keller!"

Jon pushed back his chair, setting down his half-finished roll. "I'll saddle up."

"I'm going, too," was repeated at the same time by all the Stands at the table, except the grandparents, who were getting up in age.

Each Stand saddled up his or her own horse for an evening ride to old Mrs. Keller's. She had been on oxygen for the past year. It had been brought over from the hospital as needed, but of late, she was using it every day. She'd been given batteries for backup on the days when the power grids were turned off. Amongst the evening crickets' songs, they found her outside, sitting on her porch wrapped in a blanket.

"What are you doing here?" she called. "Is there something wrong?"

Marlene called back as she dismounted. "We came because the electricity has now stopped, Mrs. Keller." Sprinting up the porch steps, she asked, "What are you doing out in this cold?"

"It's not too cold outside. I am sitting, enjoying the night noises. Ya know, if it weren't for all these night sounds—just listen to them." She leaned her head back and rocked, then added, "It would be dead quiet and pretty eerie."

She shifted, folding her nearly transparent hands in her lap and fixing her gleaming eyes on Marlene. "I know why you're here, Marlene, and don't worry about me. I'll be fine for a day, and we will see how the Lord handles the rest."

"You should move to our house, Mrs. Keller. The men can move your things over first thing in the morning."

"Nope, it's not going to happen. I'm not moving to your place, dear, or anywhere else." She squeezed Marlene's hand. "Don't you think I have been aware of this day for some time?" She rocked back and forth and then looked at Adam, her gaze piercing, even as her thin blue lips curved upward. "My goodness, Adam, you're such a handsome young man. Have you found yourself a young lady yet?"

"No, Mrs. Keller, not yet." He chuckled and offered a wink. "God says I'm too good-looking and He can't find me a fit. But I hear you've come in a close second so far."

"Oh, you're such a scoundrel." She giggled. "Marlene, you take your family home tonight. I'll be fine till tomorrow. I know what's coming and want to spend the time alone, talking things over with Him. You can stop by tomorrow, and then we'll talk."

Each of the Stands stepped over the long plastic oxygen line on the floor and kissed her, telling her to go inside soon. She promised and then said she'd sit there a bit and enjoy the sight of all of them riding away on horses—a sight she never thought she'd see, but now she wanted to watch as if a good old movie came to life.

The next day, Adam rode with his mom back over to Mrs. Keller's bright and early to do any chores and then to convince her to move.

"Nope, not going to go today." She took a couple of deep breaths. "I talked it over with the Good Lord, and He said I don't have to go. Now, I am cutting down the amount I use and how often, so I…" She coughed a couple of times. "I can stretch this out to three days, at least."

"I see I can't get you to change your mind, Mrs. Keller, though you should consider moving now." Marlene cocked her head to the left, peering hard as if to see if Mrs. Keller might reconsider it. "Well, this I won't take this for a no. Mrs. Keller, we will be doing the chores and cooking your meals so you won't use any more oxygen than necessary. You sit back and take it easy."

The day was mixed with chores, people visiting, naps, and even some laughter. But, that night, she still wouldn't budge, and without her, they went home.

In the morning, she coughed even more, using her oxygen only once an hour for fifteen minutes, during which, her color would bounce back. That night, she set her alarm to sleep only two hours. Then she would turn the oxygen off for a while. She insisted, saying at her age she was up and down anyway, and then she could talk to God.

The third day, when she went to bed it would be the last of her oxygen. Sometime in the first hour of sleep, her oxygen would stop pumping. Mrs. Keller told them she wanted to talk to the Lord as she took her last breath, in her own bed.

The Stands honored her final wish, and they stood and prayed with her, turning her over to God. They left her talking to Yahweh of things only the two knew.

In the morning, Marlene and the three Stands daughters went to the house to prepare and wash the body. It had become the practice of true friends and close relatives. The fancy caskets and all the rules of burying had been cast aside. Then the men would show up after hours of digging. This job was done as soon as possible—no refrigeration or embalming being the deciding factor.

Personal preference of where had been discussed ahead of time. Mrs. Keller had asked to be next to her husband's grave on a piece of property the town owned. It overlooked the entire town, giving a feeling of ancestors looking down at the town they loved.

"What if she is still alive, Momma? I've heard a body can go on, undetected," asked Beth, Marlene's youngest daughter, now thirty-seven.

"Kally will be heading over in a while. She'll be sure for us. But, believe me, *you'll* be able to tell, and I will explain and show *you* what to do."

No more was to be said about why she would need to know this impending job. A new homeschool lesson was about to begin again.

When they arrived, they boiled water, gathered towels, and then walked into Mrs. Keller's bedroom. There, Mrs. Keller lay, her mouth still open, pursed as if she'd gone the way she'd wanted to, talking to God. They took the moment in.

Then the body opened one eye, lips quirking. "What's the matter? Did I disappoint you?"

Marlene and Kally jumped. Catching her thoughts in a second, Marlene said, "You just scared the life out of me, Mrs. Keller." She pressed a hand to her own leaping heart. "How are you doing?"

"Weak, very weak, but I still can talk to the Lord without using my voice." She wheezed with every breath.

This went on, day after day, for a week. And every day, Mrs. Keller *was* stronger than the day before. When Adam rode home with Marlene on the seventh day, they talked about how well Mrs. Keller was doing.

"Adam, what do you make of her doing so well?"

"Well, since she's still talking to God, I guess, He doesn't want to interrupt her."

Marlene started giggling. Then they both couldn't stop laughing. Then she did something her son had never seen her do: she shouted out Psalms 150.

CHAPTER 18

AND THEY CRIED OUT!

By the time Adam turned thirty-nine, the Stands home had shrunk from the sad losses of both Grandma and Grandpa Clip and also Grandma Stands. It started a new era, causing Jon and Marlene to look at themselves differently. *They* were now the oldest in this family.

They both spoke of it only one time. Then, as an unspoken pledge, they never brought it up again. They just faced that they were at the top rung of the family ladder.

Spring took her by surprise. Marlene sat at the kitchen table, dreading what she had heard. Her elbows braced on the table, and her hands clasped together, holding her head up under her nose, covering her mouth. She had to think. She shifted to read her husband's face. When one had been married that long, it was all one needed to do to read the other's thoughts.

"Momma, I know this comes as a shock to you. We have prayed and prayed. But both of us come back to it, and we are called to do it."

Marlene faced her youngest daughter, Beth, and her husband, Kyle. They had always given her and Jon peace, never any trouble. Kyle was such a good son-in-law, he reminded Marlene of Psalm 1: *He delighted in God's ways and never did go the way of sinners.* Not once could she remember him doing anything foolish. But now, at their age, going out on faith into this world only to minister as a traveling evangelist… in this day and age? This announcement was so sudden, and her heart didn't want them to leave—no, she wanted all her children around her. With no phones and no real mail anymore, she might never hear from them again. But she listened.

"So, tell us how you plan all this. What *has* God been leading you to do?"

"First, Momma, I must tell you about the dream Kyle had. It was fall. Oh, it was all so powerful and clear. In the dream, he saw hundreds of people wandering all around, not knowing which way to go. Some ran into trees, and some walked into different dangers. You know? Like they were blind, running into everything. God spoke up from the heavens to Kyle, saying, 'There are many still who cannot see the way. Where are those Shepherds of mine? I need Shepherds out with the lost sheep!'

"That same night, Momma, I had a dream. Only, in my dream, I helped a Shepherd, and I was feeding people."

"Why didn't you tell me about this?"

"Because," Kyle spoke up, "we still needed to test this to be sure it was from God. We knew if this was His doing, He would supply *all* the ways and means."

"How are you going do this?"

"So Kyle and I can travel in comfort and carry what we need, he has built a portable home, which his mules will pull. Almost like those fancy RVs." Beth laughed. "I worked on the storage of food, water, and necessary things from clothing, sewing, medical, and such. We've also been collecting extra Bibles to pass out."

"What about food? It will run out."

"God will be the one who will have to take care of us then, Momma."

Jon had said nothing during this time, but now, he spoke up. "I see."

Each one was quiet as if these two were teenagers running out in life instead of a couple in their forties.

Jon crossed his arms, leaning back in his chair. "Can I see this mule-pulled RV of yours?"

"Sure, Dad. It's over in the Thomases' old barn." A gleam lit Kyle's eyes like a man about to show off his prize bull at the state fair. He pushed back his chair and started to the door.

Marlene met her husband's gaze, and they shared a grin over his boyish exuberance, just as they would have were he their son beginning to walk. Then Jon set his hand to the small of her back and gestured to the door. "After you, sweetheart."

She leaned back into his hand as they followed the children to where they were holding their prize.

As the barn doors opened, light gave life to his wonder. The hookup for the mules stood on blocks giving this creation a picture of what it would look like.

"Come on, Momma. I'll show you the inside. It may not be big, but that's a lot less work to clean. The steps are over here, and they aren't too steep."

Jon grinned while his wife and daughter wasted no time going inside.

"Sir?" Kyle gestured to show him the outside workings. "I was able to salvage parts from here and there and put them all together." His lips curved upward to a proud grin. "Ultimately, you've got to admit, she turned out pretty sharp." The men went over every working part, including the roof.

"Constructed from tile left in Mr. Tarsh's barn, it'll reflect the sun." Kyle rapped the roof with his knuckles. "No matter how hot the atmosphere gets, the tile won't heat to the touch. And these—they're two-way mirrors from the old police station. Kinda nifty, huh? We'll be able to see out, but the mirrors just reflect the sun, so neither it nor anyone else can see in. Over here, I vented in a stove for heating, with proper vents for fumes. And Beth found a roll-out awning to shelter a 'porch' when we're stopped—she even made Velcro screens to keep out bugs!"

His son-in-law's obvious pride and admiration of his wife warmed Jon's heart. The boy would take good care of her out there—not that he'd ever doubted.

"How light is this thing?" asked Jon, wondering about the mules.

"I don't know exactly, but I tried to make it light, yet sturdy. I've tested it plenty of times with only minor corrections. From my calculations on the weight of everything we need—tools, food—overall, it should be about 2000 pounds. I kept it as light as I could by using things like foam for insulation, and the sink is plastic. The only heavy part is the frame. I took a lot of ideas from all the travelers we met, including the group with the Conestogas. My mules will be fine." He stopped, paused, and changed the subject. "Jon, if we can't make a go of it, we *will* head back." He touched Jon's arm, reassuring him he was not so prideful as not to head back if things got tough.

"So"—Jon nodded—"when are you planning to go?"

"Next week. I like it being early spring, so the mules will have time to adjust before it gets hot."

"Which way are you heading?"

"West, south, whatever roads are open will direct us to go or stop."

The week was full of everyone giving ideas of what to take or what to leave.

Marlene had the most unusual request of all. While she and Beth were going over things in the wagon's small kitchen, she turned to Beth. "I would like to ask a favor of you both."

"Sure, Mom, if we can do it. What is it?"

"I would like to ask if Adam could ride along with you for a while. He knows the roads and can guide you two to what you're seeing, and when you and Kyle feel comfortable, you can send him home. Is that okay?"

Beth sat on the chair by the table, tapping her head with a wooden spoon. "Mom, that's a great idea. Have you talked it over with Adam?"

"Not yet. But he loves to go out there, anywhere, and whenever anyone asks him to go look for things. I can only ask him if it's okay with you two."

"Kyle will be back soon, and I'll ask him. But I don't think he would object."

"I sure would feel better. Not that I don't trust God, but *I* would feel better."

Adam had no problem saying yes to the chance to go along, and he started packing in his mind before the conversation finished. *Should I ride my horse and pack to camp, or should I take a wagon in case I find something? No one needs anything right now. My horse it is.*

Most of Tipperville turned out to say so long to Beth and Kyle and Adam. One of the older farmers, Joe Rupert, gave the couple a gift that surprised and intrigued the whole bunch of them. It was a cage—including feed—for seven homing pigeons. He provided instructions for their care and feed as well as a book with little tubes, explaining how to send them back to Tipperville. A letter system.

"Oh, Mr. Rupert, this is the answer to my parents' prayers. Do they have names?"

"Yep, and they know them, too. Well, maybe they don't know their names, but I gave them names according to their personalities. See, this one is the biggest—he's Brutus. He pushes everyone out of the way to take the feed, but because he's so strong, you could use him for the longest distance."

"Now, it's best to release them in the earliest part of the morning, just after the sun rises." He straightened, puffing his chest like a proud parent whose kids just graduated from college with straight A's. "Oh, and don't send them off in a storm. If the weather is good, they can fly up to five hundred miles a day. So, use them wisely, and your family and I will enjoy the news."

"Thank you so much!" Beth hugged Mr. Rupert.

"Listen, this is what they're bred for, and I will be tickled pink to see them at work. Just read the book. I underlined a few parts to take note of, but you should be fine."

With that, they hooked the cage to the side of the wagon. The pastor gathered Kyle and Beth together and anointed them with oil and prayer.

As the wagon pulled away, Adam rode ahead on his mare, He imagined the only thing those waving bye could see from the back was the chicken cages riding off with a goat.

CHAPTER 19

GOD DIDN'T CHANGE HIS MIND ABOUT YOU

On their third day out, a storm rumbled in, bringing a change in barometric pressure. They stopped and secured everything, from animals to the portable home. Once back inside, cozy and warm, they played cards and read. Everything fared fine, leaving them more confident in what they were doing.

Every once in a while, Adam was able to show them a road that was no longer used just by looking at the lay of the land. He also taught them how to judge the sturdiness of a bridge.

Whenever they came to an area where someone or some*ones* lived, they would introduce themselves. Then they would tell the people what they were doing and ask if there was anything with which they could help. Some accepted and then sent them on with blessings. Some rejected.

One old man with only one leg asked for assurance of salvation. He thanked the three when they were leaving, teasing that, before they came, he wasn't sure he had a leg to stand on with God, but now he understood.

The day for Adam to head back came way too quickly for Beth, and she started to weep. "Oh, Adam, it's hard to say goodbye. I wish you would be able to stay on with us. But I know Mom would kill me if I talked you into it."

He hugged her hard. "I would love to stay, Sis. Who knows, maybe we can meet up again. You never know what God has in mind, do you?"

"No, that's for sure." She shook her head and gazed at Kyle, who was now hugging her to support her.

"Tell your parents we'll send the first pigeon in about two weeks, then once a month."

Adam turned his horse, waved, and then headed home. This return trip would be a shorter ride since he was by himself.

The last night before he could reach home, Adam saw a sturdy stone ranch house. He gathered by the looks it was no longer used. He had not noticed it before. Judging by the grass and weeds, it had been vacant maybe six months to a year.

It beckoned to his curiosity and could provide shelter for the night. Never before had he considered someone's old home, but he shivered from rain in the air.

After investigated enough to be sure no one lived there, he walked through a side door into the kitchen. A note rested on the kitchen table. Knowing it wasn't for him, he didn't read it. He checked out the rest of this small one-story home, finding little more than two chairs and one made-up bed in the only bedroom before his curiosity bested him. Picking up the folded tent-shaped paper, he read it.

> Dear whoever is in my home, I can no longer stay by myself and have gone to live with a friend. The bed has fresh sheets, and you are welcome to stay. God has told me to leave it this way so you would feel welcomed. Sign your name and make the bed for the next person.
> A friend in Jesus.

A smile softened his expression, his shoulders relaxing. He stooped over the table and added his name below the signature.

Outside, he took care of his horse and brought in his bedroll and supplies. Feeling at home, he fixed up a small dinner and then listened to the rain morph into a heavy downpour. He couldn't locate a lantern, but he unearthed some old plates to place his makeshift candle on.

On the floor in the bedroom closet, he discovered three books. One was to his liking, an old Western. *Well, this is a nice find.* He sat and read till his mind didn't comprehend was he was reading, and then he headed for bed. He refused to use the sheets and pillow, so he rolled out his bedroll and pillow, blew out his candle, and slept. And he dreamt.

Golden sunshine warming him, Adam stood in a field. Three men huddled about twenty feet from him. Each was giving directions to a rock. One said, "This is the way for a rock." Another claimed, "That way is not the way, but head this way." And the last exclaimed, "Listen to me! I know what is right!"

That rock just sat, unmovable.

The three walked off.

Then Adam approached the rock and squatted to take a closer look. When he did, the rock opened its eyes, and it looked sad. He brought the rock to his chest and woke up.

The rising sun pooled light beside his makeshift bed, helping him remember where he was. *What a dream!* All that day, it played in his mind over and over.

About three o'clock, he was riding down the home stretch to Tipperville. He began to see fallen trees and branches. *Wow, they must have had a good storm while I was gone.* He studied the turning color of the wood's flesh and the crushed terrain around it, noting it must have happened a while ago. *Hope everything's okay.*

He quickened his horse.

His horse stood at the edge of Stands' property, and before him spread nothing but devastation. *Where are the cattle and horses? Where are the barns?* He rode at full gallop. Reaching the house, he jumped down off his horse and ran inside. There at the kitchen table was his neighbor, Mrs. Rupert. Her face hid nothing.

"What happened?"

"Oh, Adam, it's been bad. Sit down."

Feeling the grief from her, he was not sure he could take it.

"A couple of days after you three left, there was a storm. It produced several tornadoes."

"Where are my mom and pa?"

"Your mom is lying down, and your dad is... Well, he's out in the back by the small barn—the only one left. Everything else is gone, including the animals."

She spoke so quietly and slowly he knew there would be more. "It was the day your brothers and sisters, along with their families, were all over at Dan's house for Kally's birthday party. Your parents were about to head over when the tornadoes struck. Dan's house was another place one touched down." She looked deep into his eyes. "They're gone, Adam, all of them."

Adam's head swirled. He thought he'd pass out. Hank came in just in time, apparently having seen Adam's horse wandering in the yard. Then they explained what had happened at Dan's home. His mom was in bed in a grief-stricken shock, and his pa?

"I've got to go see Pa!"

"Wait! There's more."

Adam stopped, even as tears ran down his face. He turned a pleading look on them. *No, not more!*

"Sit and let me finish."

He *had* to sit as his legs were giving out. Hank tried to give him some whiskey, but Adam, remembering his pledge, said, "No, thank you." He inhaled a big breath. "Go on."

"When we all gathered at the grave site, your father decided it was his place to speak. He was silent for the longest time, then put his hat in his hands. The only thing he said was 'I turn my children back to God, where all things come from. To God, I give the Glory.'

"Afterward, your mother took to her bed. With her grief and age, well, it's been rough on her."

"Should I go to her now?"

"No, please, let me finish."

Adam cringed.

"A few days later, your dad cleaned up the barns, to see what he could salvage. He was picking up debris, but not being as careful as he should. That old combine tractor had been tipped over on its side. He was up by the cabin when a beam shifted. One window exploded with such force that the safety glass embedded in his body from top to bottom. It even went through his clothes."

She dabbed at her eyes. "He won't let us try to work on him, Adam. He just sits out back and picks at the areas on his own. I don't know if he's even gotten any out." That said, she wept, unable to tell anymore.

Adam stood, thanked them both, and then walked out back to find his father.

Jon sat by a burning pit, throwing scraps of wood into it from the barns. Scabs pitted his face and arms, flaming an infectious red. Adam had never before seen his father in shorts. His legs carried the same condition, and judging by the loose shirt, his chest suffered the same.

When Jon saw Adam, his bloodshot eyes wept. He made sure Adam would not touch him because of all the glass. They sat staring into the fire for the longest time, unable to speak.

Then Jon brought himself to start in a low voice. "Everything hit so hard and fast. I have tried to keep my thoughts right with God." He wiped an eye. "After the funeral and my accident, I thought I was at my lowest. Then three friends of mine came over to be supportive, and supportive they weren't." Anger mottled his already red and swollen face.

"I couldn't believe it, Adam. They analyzed why all this happened to me. None of it was right, not one bit of it. More or less they accused me of having done something wrong in God's eyes and claimed I needed to ask God for forgiveness, to get in His blessings again." He grunted. "I don't want to talk about them anymore."

Yet in seconds, he continued. "One thing I do know, Adam, is God never changes. He never changes His mind about you. He doesn't love you one minute and then curse you the next."

Adam thought of his dream and remembered the three men giving bad directions to a rock.

"It was right of you to stand firm with them. Pa, I'm proud of you." He told his father about his dream. They discussed the friends. Adam and his father figured the only way to feel better about them was to pray for them. As their spirit moved, they went right into worshiping God together for a long time. This was what they both needed. When they were done, they left the burn pit and went in to see Marlene.

She lay in her bed. When she saw Adam and Jon together, she cried out. "Jon, I'm so sorry! I am so weak. Seeing you get hurt was the last straw. You, of all men, don't deserve any of this." She peered into Jon's face and pushed herself up to him. "I have to tell you, I have sinned. In my heart, I came to the point where I wished you could curse God and die. I am so sorry I couldn't take your suffering." She wept. "I couldn't. I just couldn't!"

"Shh, shh." He patted her head and then kissed her hair. "God has not changed His mind about us, Marlene. He is *not* that kind of God. He still loves us. Now, let's go to work on this glass."

In the following weeks, friends came from all over to rebuild the barns, bring extra animals for gifts, and supply everything from tools to grain, proving more than the Stands ever could use.

CHAPTER 20

WHERE ARE THE WALLS?
WHERE ARE GOD'S WAYS?

Beth and Kyle traveled for weeks. Collapsed bridges or downed trees, rocks—anything that could hinder—turned them this way and that way. But they trusted God, knowing He would get them where He wanted them to be. Their hearts were light, and Beth worked on a code she could send home with the next pigeon so those who read it could figure out what she was saying.

A goal of theirs was to head on over to a town where they remembered one of Kyle's relatives lived, if she was still alive. Aunt Esther, a delightful woman, had written many a time about living in such a nice Christian town. Stories in her letters of God's doings had delighted the family every time. Very long ago. She'd be about eighty-five now.

The mules did a wonderful job, and those who had horses wished they had converted to mules, seeing how well they traveled and did chores. They used less food and water. Their health far surpassed those horses, and where a horse could walk into danger, a mule would never go. If they took good care of a mule, it could live to be fifty. Kyle watched over his mules and put them up against the trailer at night to keep an ear to the sounds.

One night, Beth snuggled against his side, a cool cup of water in her hand. "I've been thinking. Maybe we should get ourselves a dog. I know we'd have to figure out about food, but with the way some men look at our mules, a noisy guard dog would give us a better night's sleep."

"I've been rolling it around myself. The last house we were at? I think the only reason that man listened to us was so he could check out our mules. He tried everything he could to talk me out of them."

"If you noticed, after you said no the last time, his neck blotched with anger. He kept saying he wanted them for his son, who I never saw."

"Well, my mules work only with a kind hand, and with his hard way about him, they would never move one foot. Let's forget about him and try to get some sleep."

The next day, about half a mile after they started out, a hand-painted sign promised they only had ten miles to go to his aunt's town. The road was fairly good, still short grass and smooth, so if it stayed this good, they could make it that day.

At noon, they stopped to eat and walk around, enjoying their daily time to stretch and care for the mules and goat.

As Kyle went out for a run, Beth ambled up a hillside that greeted her with early wildflowers. Everything nowadays had so much overgrowth that she liked to walk through open areas when there was one. After climbing for a while, she found a long, flat rock to sit on and enjoy the view.

She had no idea she was being followed. He was not far away at all. Dirty, thin, he thought of nothing but her. He liked her. Ever since he had seen her three days ago, his thoughts had been of nothing but her, and today, he'd make his move.

Beth never noticed him. He was sneaking up on the other side of the rock. He took the chance and leaned his body against hers.

She thought Kyle joined her—until she *smelled* him. She turned to look behind her, and he kissed her. Her heart jumped. She froze, then jolted back, and studied his eyes. She softened while falling in love. He was a dog—a German shepherd, to be exact.

"Well, let's hope you're still friendly after that kiss."

His ears lay back in a submissive way. He lowered his head and blinked. Then he lay down and whined. He was about a year old, maybe, and thin. By the way he acted, he must have belonged to someone.

Reaching out her hand, she stroked the top of his head with two fingers, then with her full hand. With that, he placed his head in her hand. The two became one.

"You must be hungry." From her pocket, she pulled out a piece of jerky she'd stashed for a snack later. *Here goes the test.* She handed him the piece, and gently, as though careful not to scare her, he took it.

Beth walked back to the trailer with her new companion. Kyle was still out on his run. She sniffed her hand and tried to figure a way to bathe the new member. With food to coax him, she succeeded, and all they needed now was sunshine to finish the dry job.

The new member rolled in the grass and ran about, as happy as could be. Settling at her feet, he panted. His adoring expression saying he couldn't stop his love for her.

Kyle came back from his run and, not noticing the new member, readied the mules and then the goat. He called out, asking if she had everything.

"Yep, sure do." She was on the other side of the wagon, and as she hopped up to sit with Kyle, so did the new member, scaring the life out of Kyle as he took a place on the seat between them.

"What is that? Who is that?"

"That is God's gift to me—or I should say—us."

"Where did it come from?"

Beth told the story.

Kyle smiled. "God sure works in strange ways. Is it a he or she?"

"He. I keep calling him Boy. What do you think we should call him?"

Kyle tipped his head, as though thinking for a while, studying the new member sitting between them, who was having the time of his life riding. The dog's eyes tilted back and forth, looking at both of them. "Boy. Since this is the closest we'll ever get to have a son—and he is a gift from God —let's just call him Boy." And Boy he was.

Kyle drove them into the small town of Salem, the place purported to be such a lovely Christian town. Instead, they entered a rundown shantytown. The town stood built on a grid around a small square block, displaying evidence of a great fire. Nothing remained but piles of burnt stone and brick. They asked an older woman walking what had happened and if she knew of his aunt. She hugged her coat to her as if fearful they'd try to steal it till they mentioned Esther.

Then the woman loosened her hold and offered a curt nod. "Esther lives about a half-mile from here. Take the next street left and follow it till you see a two-story brick house with a cross in the front yard. It will be on the right. You can ask her about the fire." She walked away, obviously not wanting to talk anymore.

"Brr," said Beth. "I hope they're not all that cold."

Pulling up to a brick two-story house, they avoided the chickens running over the yard, plucking at debris here and there. A thin worn path led to a side door. Beth waited with Boy while Kyle went and knocked.

"Yesss?" said an old, skinny woman, the *S* catching in a whistle through missing teeth. Watery round eyes blinked beneath a woolen scarf holding back wisps of white hair.

"Are you Esther Russ?"

"I am."

"I'm your nephew, Kyle."

"Goodness! What are you doing here?" Her thin face crinkled into a vibrant smile.

"My wife and I are traveling and ministering. We decided, while we were in the area, we'd look you up."

"Well, come on in." She opened the door wider with an arm as thin as her cane.

"Let me take care of my animals, and then we will be in." Kyle explained what he'd seen to Beth.

"Stay, Boy."

As if he understood, Boy listened to Kyle and sat, staring at the door where they entered Aunt Esther's home.

Beth eased into a hardback kitchen chair. Mere feet away, separated only from the kitchen by a line where aged tile met an old rug, was a room with Esther's only chair of comfort and a small bed. End tables and shelves held precious memories. Although neat, dirt and dust lurked in crevasses and surfaces, evident to one with good eyes.

Esther's dinner, an egg and a biscuit, lay uneaten on a plate beside Beth.

"I would offer you something to eat, but I can't seem to find enough eggs of late. I think some of the neighbors may be needing them."

"Oh, Aunt Esther, don't you worry. In fact, we were going to ask if you'd like to have dinner with us tonight. Weren't we, Kyle?"

"Sure, Beth is a good cook, and I caught a fat rabbit yesterday. We had it soaking in salt till today. You don't mind rabbit, potatoes, and carrots do you?"

Beth's eyes looked up before her head moved, and a stunned look of "you got to be kidding me" turned into a big smile. "That sounds so good! My dear, I haven't had anything but what comes out of the back end of a chicken for, well, I don't remember last."

"That's been *all* you've had to eat?" asked Beth.

"About that. I don't have much. This last winter used up what I did have, and that weren't that much in the first place."

"Good gracious, Kyle! God got us here just in time. Aunt Ester, I saw you had milk on the table. Do you have a goat?"

"Nope. Someone or something took my only goat left, and I had just found out the dear thing was pregnant." She sighed. "But I do have something people want, and that has been able to keep some food and milk on the table, even wood for cooking."

Grinning, she sighed and looked toward the ceiling. "See, years ago, a young woman came through this town and taught me, 'If you don't have a man to help, then buy up as much as you can of these two things, and your neighbors will always trade for them.' " She chuckled now and rubbed her delicate hands together. "She was right! They have been the only thing keeping me alive." Then she lowered those hands to the table, a tremor quaking through them. "But this town changed after the fire. They have gotten a sad spirit about them."

Kyle leaned forward, laying his hand atop her cold fingers. "How did the fire happen? We saw the area."

Beth interrupted before she could answer, excusing herself to go prepare dinner and check on her Boy. As she opened the side door to go out, there Boy lay curled up, waiting. Oh, he had her heart. When she went to the wagon, she invited him in while she cooked, testing out his manners, and he passed the test.

Dinner was served in the trailer, and Aunt Esther's eyes weren't larger than her stomach. She could eat! Her belly bulged like that of a fat young pup. Kyle helped her back to the house after dinner, then tended to the animals and came in for the night.

After they stepped over Boy for the third time, he started to complain. When Boy went to the door to be let out, he was panting and preferred the cooler outside. Kyle followed him out and then found an old box in his aunt's shed, which he put between the door and mules. Kyle then placed his seat cushion in it. "Thanks for choosing us, Boy." He patted the dog's head and went inside.

Beth puttered about, getting ready for bed. "Hey, how about telling me all about that fire in town?"

"The whole thing is pretty strange. First, Aunt Esther told me about that woman she spoke of earlier. Years ago, a young woman came in, trying to help the town prepare for the future. It was going along great till she had to move on."

Sitting on the side of the bed, Kyle propped up a pillow and leaned back. "Right after that, she told me a couple of wealthy farmers moved here and bought up most of the land. Slowly, they had the people working for them. The townspeople never met or noticed either of the men's wives. One of the men married a woman who was maybe Muslim. The other man was married to an atheist, so neither man had any love for God."

At that, he rubbed his forehead and tried to recall the next point. "In no time, they had taken over everything, controlling the whole makings of the town and its people. Salem, in time, relied on them for everything. Because the two men had no respect for the church—or God—they spread the people farther and farther from the church."

Beth lifted one hand in a fist. "Not Esther, though. She honored God and had nothing to do with them. You saw her cross."

He nodded. "It happed that, one month before the fire, the town's pastor passed away. After that, the church and everything around it burnt to the ground. No one knows how it started, but Esther figures it was by the hand of those two."

Beth was on her side, listening intently to every word.

Kyle settled beside her and tucked her under his arm. "She said, with the minister gone and the church gone, the people weakened even more, and they never did recover. Oh, and the two men established a store in town, where the people have to trade work for food and other stuff."

Beth reached to turn off the light.

In silence, holding each other. He kissed her good night and tried to sleep.

In the morning, while Beth prepared breakfast, Kyle tapped a pencil on the table. Then he rolled it around, back and forth on the tabletop.

She stopped what she was doing and sat, lifted his chin, and looked him in the eye. "Well, whatcha thinking?"

"God needs us here, Beth. First, I need to snoop around and check things out. But I do feel this was God's doing, to get us here. This place needs to be rebuilt, spiritually and physically."

"Plus," she added. "Your aunt needs a lot of help, especially in the food department." With his brows pinched and lowered, his lips pressed tight, she could see his mind was running at high speed. Taking his hands in hers, she said, "We had better pray right now and be sure God's ahead of us and not behind us."

That day, Esther agreed to Beth's suggestion to spring-clean her home. She was warned she wasn't needed up the stairs. Beth worked the next few days washing windows and walls. Anything there got a good scrubbing. The cooking was switched to inside the house to help heat the old woman's home and dry things out.

On the fifth morning, two women about Beth's age came by toting a cart piled high of cut and split wood. They proceeded to stack the wood by

Esther's side door. Esther greeted them, took from them two cloth bags, then continued to the forbidden curtain at the base of the upstairs. Upon returning, she handed their bags back to them—their now-bulky bags. She gave both a hug and then started an introduction.

"Girls, I'd like you to meet my nephew's wife, Beth. They will be staying here for a while."

Both smiled lightly, rechecking their work as they took one more glance around at the cleaned room. Then they nodded and started leaving. Even though they were in their forties, hard work had aged their looks. But Beth was not about to lose a chance to talk to them, speaking up, "How far did you have to tote that load of wood?"

The women both stopped and turned to her. One swept her black ponytail over her shoulder, then slid a hand into her Levi's pocket. Raggedy strings from the cuffs of well-worn jeans tangled with grungy shoelaces as she shuffled sneakers that might have been white once. "We've had to pull this load from about"—intelligence and self-assurance rumbled through her voice before she paused to calculate—"I'd say, three miles. Don't you think so, Millie?"

Now Millie also wasn't as quiet as she first put out. "It felt like fifty, but it was about three." She looked at Beth's home. "How do you like living in that?"

"I like it. It's small inside, but comfy. Kyle—my husband—and I have only traveled about a month now." A month? Goodness, it was time to send off a pigeon. "Come on in. I'll show you the place."

Just as God planned it, a friendship blossomed.

CHAPTER 21

THEY HAVE NOT BECAUSE THEY ASK NOT!

Each morning, Kyle led his animals to public land for grazing, taking the opportunity to check out the people and the town. As he asked around, he heard no plans for a new minister.

The men avoided talking about God, and the women worked so hard they had no time to look to God. The people nicknamed the two men in charge of the town the "Landlords." During the first few years, they bought up much of the land. Without land, the people had nothing left to do but work for this group. Then the Landlords took over the general store, arranging it so, when the people worked for them, they could trade for supplies. They ran the people without the people knowing it. Years later, the people lost the ability to take care of themselves without this arrangement and became slaves. They could do nothing but continue working for the two men. The ones who worked the fields were the only people allowed to know and do only that one job. One didn't know how to do another's job. These slick men took away the townspeople's ability to be independent.

One man told Kyle, "I'm fifty-five, and I know nothing about planting. I only milk cows. My dad is still working at the same farm in the water supply group. My wife cooks for one home, only the breakfast time. Put that all together, and you can see we have to continue working for them, for our bread and butter. And that is my sister's department, the butter department."

Yes, surely, this looked great to the people at first. But they were not only tricked: they were held captive.

CHAPTER 22

YOU ARE A DISGRACE, SALEM! *REBUILD?* REBUILD!

Kyle had prayed about what to say to inspire these people to change, to seek God again, and to rebuild their church. With God's help, he gathered all the families at the old town hall on Sunday. Many of them came out of curiosity, to listen to what this man of God had to say.

He shared how he knew about this town, how he found it to be in physical and spiritual ruin. Then he expressed their need to turn back to their first love, God, and rebuild the church. Without argument, they *all* replied, "Let us then rebuild!"

In the back of the room stood three brothers—Sam, Toby, and Gus—at the door, men close to the Landlords. "What are you trying to do? Take over this town?" they accused.

Kyle looked at them, not saying anything for a moment. "This is God's town, God's people, not mine. And the way I see it, He doesn't need your help."

They walked out.

The townspeople showed up every day for the work assignments, in perpetual organized shifts, yet they didn't stop working for the Lords. Sam, Toby, and Gus relentlessly mocked and ridiculed those working.

Sam yelled out, "Hey, you! Mike Zee! You have never built anything in your life. You think you can do this kind of work? The way you're doing it is all wrong. It's gonna fall just as soon as a fox leans against it.

But I suppose all those years of making butter and cheese has taught you how."

Toby and Gus daily tried to unrest the people. "Since those stones are already charred, why not throw a bunch of sacrifice on them to see if God will zap it done in one day? You all are so stupid you don't even know not to use the same burnt rocks to make the base."

Kyle was tired of it. He prayed, "O Lord God, those three are mocking You and Your work. We don't need to listen to these fools running their mouths every day. Please don't let this go on. I know You see their sin. Can You please do something with them? I wish You would have them hauled away. I'm afraid the people might quit building Your church."

With all the harassment, those who worked on the church walls went on working even harder. Soon, they completed half the walls.

Steven Orson paced his marble foyer, his hands fisting at his sides. Wasn't often something made him mad—or was he afraid? The very idea of the latter angered him yet further. He was not afraid.

Not of some ignorant rubes getting together and playing in the rubble.

The front door opened, and the soles of his loafer squeaked as he pivoted on his heel toward it. Kaden Hardy stood there, removing his coat with a deliberate calm that could only mean he was as upset as Steven was.

"You heard where they're sneaking off to after work each day." It wasn't a question. Of course, Kaden knew. Steven didn't offer to take the coat from his fellow "Landlord."

"Yep." Kaden shook out the folds of his leather jacket, a vintage piece that was his pride and joy, before hanging it on the hall tree. "After everything we have done for them. What do they think they need a church or a God for? Are they planning anything else other than building a stupid church?"

"Not that I know of, but my men are staying close." Steven walked to the window and surveyed the realm before him. A kingdom he'd created and would not lose. This was more than an act of rebellion. A church of all things... "I suspected something was going on, but I couldn't discern it. Then one of my men told me what they were up to."

"What I want to know now is if you want to join me and my men on a little visit?"

Mmm. That's what he expected from Kaden—no flinching when something had to be done. Steven gave a tight nod, not bothering to turn around. "The way I see it, if we let them have this church back, we're in trouble, and I don't want to lose any more workers. Every year, more and more are dying off, and with none to replace them, well, I need them to stay focused."

"Well then..." Kaden's words were a hiss near his ear. How had he gotten so close so fast? "Why don't we do this? We can send some of our men over to visit the walls of this church late at night and make it look like the structure collapsed. Remember when we burned the church? Eventually, they will give up just like before."

It was more than the church. That's the thing with Kaden. He saw the structure of something, never bothering to unearth its foundation. Standing there, Steven was slow in responding. "I keep hearing about this one man... a newcomer." He met his counterpart's gaze reflecting on the glass before him. "He's leading them."

Their gazes held. Easy to see the other man's thoughts reflected his own. "If breaking down the walls doesn't break their spirits, we'll have to do something."

Always action with Kaden. But action could bring about the wrong results. Steven closed his eyes and rubbed his throbbing temples. "Let me think. I don't want him to be their hero or depress the people so much they hate us. I'll get back to you unless you come up with something first."

That same day, as Kyle and Beth were serving soup to those who worked on the walls, Beth nudged him. "That group over there?"

A cluster of about ten people stood in the shade across the way. They kept looking at Kyle and talking, gesturing as if urging the oldest of their crowd forward.

"I see them."

She flashed him a smile. "Go talk to them, honey. I can handle the food line."

Sometimes this wife of his was too much. Love surging through him, Kyle bent down and kissed her forehead. "I'll be back to help soon."

But she waved him away, the potent scent of leeks and potatoes surrounding her, and bent to speak with the man holding his bowl before her.

Leaving Beth to her ministry, Kyle crossed the street and waved. "Not sure I've seen you guys around before. I'm Kyle." He offered his hand.

With one more glance at the younger men, the elder stepped forward. "Blayze Hudson. These here's my brothers and sons." He gave them another look. Two nodded back, so he took a deep breath. "See, it's like this. We haven't been by to help, but that don't mean we want to see nothing happen to no church...."

Then he explained they worked in the house of one Landlord. His brother had overheard what was being planned.

His heart pounding, Kyle gathered those who worked on the church together to share about what was going on and discuss what they were to face.

Once he finished, one of the younger volunteers stepped forward. "What right do they have to tell us what we can do on our own time?"

This wasn't the place to talk like that. Kyle held up his hand. "Well, we could debate questions like that all day, but let's handle this God's way now. First, you must remember God didn't bring you this far to be afraid and run. He is great and awesome and cares."

He made eye contact with the men whose faces most revealed their frustration and anger, and a part of him couldn't help sympathizing. These men had felt so ineffectual for so long, held captive by the Landlords. "This is what you are to do. As you work, put on the whole armor of God, that you may defeat your enemy. Gird your waist with truth. Put on the breastplate of righteousness. Cover your feet by studying the Gospel's peace. But most of all, friends, your shield will be your faith in God. Your heads have already been covered with Christ's helmet of salvation. What I want you to learn is to only to strike them with God's Word. God's Word will be your *living* sword."

Kyle held Norton's gaze the longest. The youngest in the group, Norton stared back at him for a long time before nodding. Some men had a harder time realizing their strength lay not in their bodies, but in their souls. But even Norton lowered his clenched fists and bowed his head when Kyle began the prayer. Eventually, as one, the people humbled themselves and prayed—for the first time in years—to the Living God.

The crew continued working and derived the plan on their own. Groups were to work twenty-four hours a day.

During that time, Kyle and Beth not only fed them but also taught them Scripture. When the mockers came to break them down mentally, they quoted Scripture to them until they either listened or left.

Steven closed the door after his counterpart, then stood there with one hand on the cool doorknob. "These meetings with Kaden better be over soon."

The man unsettled him.

Nightly sending his men out to destroy the walls wasn't working. Not when there was always someone ready to preach at them. He scowled. *Preaching! From those stupid people! I will end this!*

He released the doorknob and stomped to his study. Almost as unfathomable as the preaching were the excuses his men kept coming up with. As if they expected him to believe that, *every time* they left on their nightly destructive task, weird things happened. Like once, his top man's horse died while he was on it. Another time a swarm of bees stung both men and horses. It was as if… as if *God* was doing His part.

At least Kaden had agreed with his approach to destroying this rebellion. The families would suffer as the two of them raised the price of flour and supplies, forcing them to work more hours for them and stop working on that ridiculous church. He unscrewed the top of a twenty-year-old bottle of Scotch, one of the last bottles produced. As liquid gurgled into his glass, he smiled over Kaden's response—"We already have their land for farming. They've nothing else. Let's do it!"

News came to Kyle of how the Landlords were plotting to have all those who worked on the church put in a mandatory extra work time. Either that or they would raise the prices at the Lords' store. Anger rose to its full height inside Kyle. He rounded up a crew to confront the Landlords. Knowing the Landlords would be at their main farm for lunch, he took his group there. He found them dining on the pouch. His anger would not give any room to fear as he marched up the steps. "I've come to ask why you are doing this to your townspeople?"

One Landlord patted his mouth with his napkin before he spoke up. "I don't see as this is any concern of yours, preacher. The people's work hasn't been what it should be since they have been working on your silly church. So now, we have been forced to raise our prices." He spoke like a satisfied cat that ate a bird.

"That's a lie, and you know it. This whole thing is a lie! These are God's people, gentlemen, not yours!" Kyle pointed a finger in the air as if it were exclamation point. "They have worked for you faithfully for years and have not changed one way in how they work now."

Kyle walked up to the table and braced his hands on it. Leaning over them, he looked the men in the eye, not blinking. "It is you who must understand that God can at any time remove these people from you. He is more than capable of having them leave and go to a place that is ready and able to receive them." Pushing away from the table, he stood up straight. "If you don't back off, that may become a fact. As I have studied things around here, you do not even use any of the land around their homes." He backed up, turned, then faced them again. He smiled. "How about this: restore these people's land to them and any equipment you have also taken. Plus, when they are ready for it, a tenth of the stock and grain, so these folks can respectfully take care of themselves." He let a moment pass. "Or they walk."

Their expressions revealed this wasn't going at all the way the Lords themselves thought this meeting would go. In truth, it wasn't going the way he had planned. But he waited.

One Landlord held up one finger. He leaned to the other and whispered as they shook heads, tilted their heads with a lot of finger tapping, on the table, and then sat back again.

"We will do as you say," the other gave the response. They now needed the people more than the people needed them.

As Kyle went to leave, he stopped and warned the two men. "If you don't follow through and break your promise"—he took off his jacket and shook mud and dirt from it—"then God will do the same as this and shake the dirt out of your homes. And that, gentlemen, will be you."

Then men who stood with Kyle said, "Amen."

If it could only have stopped there, but when the wives of these two heard what was going to happen, anger started boiling inside them like a pot of black hate. Why? Because one of the wives' hate was already bubbling when the men had refused to perform a prayer to Allah as they butchered her meat. And the atheist woman's hate had grown as she'd seen them praying and thanking God. Nothing irritates an atheist more than happy Christians.

Secretly, the women met with Sam, Toby, and Gus. "It's time to kill Mr. Kyle."

Gus moved around the table, braced both hands on it, and bent forward, a slight leer quirking his five-o'clock shadow. "Why, murder?" he drawled, his smirk deepening. He tugged just slightly on her scarf. "Such an ugly thought, pretty lady. Don't that go against your religion?"

"He is an infidel." She swatted his hand from her, the beaded headdress jangling as he dropped it. "And it goes against Allah. I would be pleasing Allah to remove what hinders his worship."

"Hmm…" He turned to the other wife. "And what about you, Claire? Why do you want him gone?"

She walked up to him with ease, not afraid to state her case. "Don't toss morals at me." Arms crossed, head high, she leaned against the table. "I don't believe in any religion. And I don't care that they do. But I will not live my life surrounded by Christians. If their God cursed this world with no more children, I don't wish to serve Him. If there is no God, then the stupid fools sicken me."

"All well and good, ladies, but..." Gus winked and held out his open hand.

"Yeah," Sam piped up. "What's in it for us?"

Refia and Claire grinned at each other. So it would be done.

Kyle unfolded the note Toby handed him, asking him to meet with them on a certain matter. He shook his head and stuffed it in his pocket. Then he met Toby's hard brown eyes. "Tell your brothers the church building is going great, and I can't leave. Please have them tell me what they want anyway."

Those brown eyes hardened yet further. So he'd been right in his distrust.

Four more times the notes came, and each time Kyle's reply was the same. The fifth note now flapped from his trailer door. He ripped it off and opened it. Two simple sentences: "We've been hearing you still plan to take over everything and run us out of town. We are concerned about this and need to talk."

This was getting ridiculous. He stepped inside and moved to his table, grabbing a pen and sheet of paper from the cupboard as he passed. He stooped over the flat surface and scribbled his reply: "You are inventing what you are saying, and I will not meet with you."

On the way home that night, he saw a man who worked at one of the farms, he was sprinting up and then reach over for Kyle's arm. "Hey, man, hold up."

"Bruce." Kyle paused, feeling uneasy but remaining calm. "How's Emily?"

"Never mind that. You have to listen. I heard some men are on their way to kill you." Bruce's grip tightened on Kyle's arm. "I had to warn you. You'd better get yourself back to the church, lock yourself in, and hide."

Kyle wrenched his arm free, and the rush of anger leaped out at the speaker before him. "There is no way I would hide or run."

How he knew, he couldn't say, but he *knew* this guy wasn't sent by God to protect him but was hired by the wives and the three brothers. He still left to go home, trusting God.

In fifty-two days, they completed the church. Those who had opposed Kyle had to admit, it was by God's hand, for it was built in such a short time and during great conflict.

The townspeople gathered for their first church service. They wrote their names in a book to signify their love and pledge to Christ as their Savior.

At the church, the people asked Kyle to stay and be the new pastor. The ex-landlords surprisingly after a while showed up also, with confused wives. Maybe from fear, only time would tell. But not the brothers. Kyle had hope for all of them.

Beth sent her third pigeon, telling in her best shorthand and code where they were, that it was God's calling for them to be there, and that all was well.

CHAPTER 23

IF I ORDER THE WISDOM, DO I STILL NEED TO ORDER A PLATE OF GOD'S WAY?

Jon and Adam rode into the late afternoon toward their goal. This was the third year in a row that Adam decided to join, and Jon always came along. Yes, it was their time together, but when the games started, Jon, more than eighty years old, didn't have to be a spectator. He was the team coach. All through the season, Jon's mind would perk in thoughts of strategy and corrections. Pool was a fun game, but watching Adam and Shad play as a team was a big plus. That, for Jon, topped all the competing, along with its bragging rights and little wagers.

Drawing in forty-eight men from the area in teams of two, equaled out to a good time for the winter months ahead. Every summer there were the corn hole games, but this carried more science and strategy, practice and patience. As they rode up to an old unused department store, those gathered outside greeted them. After the informal greetings, all drifted on in.

Adam scanned the tables, looking over the groups. Andy Johnson, an old American history buff, put together this location. Over the years, he collected framed portraits of each president, aligning the walls from the first to the last. He called them "The Kings of America" because they reminded him of First and Second Kings in the Bible. Each had ruled this great country in his own way, for or against God, molding it into what it had become.

"Oh," Andy would add, "it was not just the Presidents, but who they surrounded themselves with that decided what they would be remembered for." Then he would sigh and shake his head.

This year, Andy had the first night's usual adjustments. Some new players had moved in, some had quit, or worse had passed on, placing Andy in charge, to fill or make up a new team. Years ago, when electricity ceased to operate, the balls began to bear shadows in low light. With men, it never hindered the game. If one had to play his shots blindfolded, with one arm tied behind his back, he would.

That night, when Jon and Adam waited in line for Adam and Shad's table to open, they studied those playing, analyzing the way they stroked their stick, spun the ball, and set it up for the next shots. Studying the competition was as much fun as the game.

When it was their turn, they thought they knew who the two were on the competing team. One they did, and the other, they'd never met before. The first was Mac, Adam's cousin, and he was walking over to introduce his new assigned partner.

"I'd like you to meet Sol Wiseman. He just moved here from Madison, Ohio, and he's my new partner. Rob's wife, Kate, broke her leg, and he's going to stay home with her till she heals."

Jon extended his hand, followed by Adam. Then Jon asked, "So, when did you move here?"

"About a month ago. I don't have any family left up north, so I came south to see if I can make it. If you know the Zimbas' old farm, that's where I'm at."

"Well, if you need some help, we could stop by sometime. I remember when we needed help when we first moved here."

"Thanks. I appreciate it."

As the game started, Jon was pleasantly surprised to see Mac's new partner was not only a good player but also a wise strategist. The first night ended up being theirs, guaranteeing the season would be interesting.

"I should have reminded you to hold back a little, till the handicap was set," Mac teased.

"I did." Sol grinned at him.

And Jon's heart gave a little thrill. Yes, the season would be interesting.

In the next four weeks, Adam's team stayed in the top spot and never lost a game. Sol got to know most of the men, and most of the men got to know him, finding Sol to be not only a man of God but also wise, following his last name.

Keeping to their word, the Stands and others in town discovered ways to slip over Sol's farm, but not just to help. They enjoyed his company, along with his stories from the north. In his stories, they found him to be wise and clever.

One story he shared with the men happened at his old church. Two couples had scheduled to meet with the pastor. They had been arguing over a situation that each threatened to leave the church. Before they were inside the pastor's office, they had put the pastor right in the middle, trying to see who he would side with. Sol was also in the hall at the time, witnessing the whole thing. He interrupted the mess and asked to speak to the pastor alone. Then he suggested to the pastor what he could do.

He told the pastor to take the couples into a small room, remind them of their salvation from Jesus, and place a Bible on the table between them. Next, he was to tell the couples, not to come out until they searched God's Word for the answer to their problem. Whoever stepped out of the door first without solving the problem would be the one in the wrong, and God would deal with them.

"What happened? What did the couples do?" asked the group of men.

"Well, what would have you have done?" was his only answer.

For weeks, the townspeople came over to Sol's farm to help as often as they could. A lot of single women came to meet this wise, good-looking man. During that time, Sol built the land around him to give God the glory and the wisdom to share it with others. People would say, "If we were back to needing a President, that's who I'd vote for. He could win without ever needing to raise campaign money!" Then they would finish it with, "What a nice, wise person."

By the fifth week, men from the pool hall gathered to watch Sol play. Even if they weren't playing, they came to see if Sol would win again.

"Adam, who are you and Shad playing against tonight?" asked Sol.

"Pat and Frank."

"Frank. He has that nice-looking daughter with the cute name, Princess. He's wanted me to ask her out. I've met her, and I'm thinking I might."

Jon was by Adam's side. He moved around him to look at Sol. "I hate to say this, son, but she's not a Christian. She is a good-looking woman, mind you, and nice. But she doesn't show any signs of faith in God."

Sol didn't reply. He just took up his stick, chalked up, and looked at the table's setup. He leaned over, positioned his fingers, then, with one stroke, broke apart the triangle, sinking two of the fifteen balls. He proceeded to remove the rest, one by one, never missing a shot. With everyone's attention on the game, the enjoyment of the skill, he controlled the rest of the night.

The next day, as Sol fed his stock, Princess rode up, surprising him. She was smiling and teasing him with eyes that spoke way more than words. He went over and helped her dismount.

"Good afternoon, Mr. Sol. My dad wanted me to stop over and drop off these clamps he borrowed."

"Thanks. I was just about to go in and have a cup of herb tea. Care to join me?" he offered the first convenient lie.

"Sure. I'd love to." And this new game began. Sol never knew he was losing.

A short time later, the two were married, even though Sol was warned. He slid into more lies, like giving excuses why she didn't attend church and saying she loved God in her own way.

In only a couple of years, Sol followed her lackadaisical ways toward God, missing more church than he attended. Then he never attended again. As he got older, he was known only for his foolish ways of following a woman all the way from Heaven to Hell.

CHAPTER 24

MURIEL AND SAM

Adam scanned the storeroom and all he had gathered throughout the years. Everything was new or nearly new. There were cooking utensils, medical supplies, clothing for different types of weather, a tent, and two kinds of sleeping bags—one for the cold and one for the warmer weather.

Adam's father passed away last month, one month after his mother's death. Now the only thing left to do was pack. He had given the house and everything in it to a friend with a good amount of family members. Because of what he had done for them, they assured him his room would always stay the same and be ready if he returned. He told them it wasn't necessary.

While Adam packed, he thought of Beth and figured she would like something belonging to their mom and pa, particularly his parents' Bibles and a few letters to Beth.

By the next day, he'd loaded the two mules and his horse. A compass hung on his neck, his map pocketed at his side, as friends came to say goodbye. Adam smiled, waved, and focused on seeing his sister and Kyle.

The roads ahead of him were either overgrown with vines or blocked by fallen trees and wires. Without the compass, he would never be able to find his way. What would have taken a car a couple of hours took days or longer. He didn't mind it because he now had something to do, somewhere to go, and maybe someone to see.

After a couple of weeks' travel as he was looking for needed water, he came upon a small town tucked away by curtains of overgrown green vines, as if forgotten in time. To his delight, as he rode in, people came from every direction waving.

"Welcome, stranger."

"What news do you have?"

"Come on down. Stretch your legs and visit."

"Are you hungry? We could fix you something to eat." They knew nothing of who he was but seemed so hungry for a visitor, they welcomed him.

The people passed word of this newcomer to the whole town. Folk gathered in and led him to where meetings were held, on picnic tables in the town center. The elderly, some with toothless smiles, grinned from ear to ear as Adam shook each and every hand. Then the men took care of his animals; women brought food from what they already had in their homes.

When all the warm greetings settled down, Adam addressed the crowd. "I want to thank you for your welcome. Do you always welcome travelers this way?"

"Sir"—an older gentleman stepped forward—"we haven't seen anyone since our state church leader visited almost two years ago."

An old woman, in a wheelchair sitting next to Adam, reached over and patted his hand. "Tell us who you are, dear, and what has brought you here?"

Adam delivered one of the most entertaining batches of stories he could drum up. He held everyone's attention—many rolling in laughter almost in tears—till they were satisfied. After a while, they all settled back down.

Without the townspeople noticing, two new riders on horseback rode up. Leaning on their saddle horns, they fixed their eyes on the people. One of the two shouted out, "Well, I know we have been gone a long time, but now, you don't even want to say hello?"

Every head turned to the riders. Everyone fell dead silent. In one cheer, they yelled out a greeting, and those who could ran over to the two.

They acted like lost children whose parents had just found them. Some even wept. Adam sat back, enjoying the sight of these folks being fussed over.

The old woman still sitting by Adam leaned closer. "Sam was our church's state-appointed overseer, appointed many years ago, with his wife, Muriel. He still takes his position seriously. He believes the difference between being a task from God and a vision is, 'A task is for the season, and a vision is for a lifetime.' To him, being an overseer wasn't a task. He and his wife travel to every church he was appointed over."

Nodding, Adam rose to greet the seventy-something couple. Red hair highlighted her soft waves, while thick, all-gray hair waved back from his high forehead and rounded cheeks. His voice, deep and rich, gave every word he spoke authority.

"Nice to meet you, Mr. Stands." The man swallowed Adam's hand in a warm clasp.

"Call me Adam. It's a pleasure to meet you and your wife. I rode in today and was greeted by these wonderful people."

A day with these people filled Adam's spirit with happiness. The townspeople continued to fuss over the three, opening a home always used for guests. Sitting on the porch, the trio savored a peaceful time to visit.

"So, if you don't mind my asking, how did you receive your calling to this ministry?" Adam leaned forward, ready for a good story.

Muriel smiled. "Sam never minds anyone asking. He feels privileged to be able to share his story."

"I was called the first time, at roughly the age of twelve. Before God spoke that there would be no more children. I was staying at our pastor's home with his family. I just about lived there. Since my parents worked, they paid the Mitchells to watch me. One night, I woke to someone calling. I thought it was the pastor. He was blind at the time from diabetes. I thought he wanted help with something, but when I came to him, he denied calling me. Three times that night I heard my name called. By the third time, I insisted the pastor might have been doing it in his sleep. Then Pastor Eli said, 'Boy, if it happens again, say, "Yes, Lord. I am Yours and I'm listening." ' It did happen again, and I did as was told." He almost whispered as he leaned forward to continue.

"Instantly, I felt the Lord's presence around me. He was standing next to me." His voice rose. "He told me He would do something soon to change the world. He said a lot of his ministers were sadly corrupted, and they would be dealt with soon. No matter what they did, nothing would appease Him. This was when many pastors and their families' sins were open to the public eye." His mouth in a frown, he shook his head, wisps of gray hair falling on his high forehead.

"That included the sons of my pastor. In my life, the heavenly Father was with me. He had told me He would lead me into battles. My job in those battles was to help His people. He showed me there would be those who didn't know His Word and were weak in their faith. But it would also turn out to be a time of great spiritual growth and preparation for believers."

Pulling at the skin under his sagging chin, he continued. "I represent a church and take my job seriously. I claim no political power. People ask, when I come to a town, if I can appoint a leader over them. But they don't need a leader. They need only to follow God, let Him be their leader. If they are able to do that, all will be well."

He settled back in his chair and crossed an ankle over the other knee. "I find myself to be more of a prophet. That's saying I have a word from the Lord to you."

"Me?"

"Yes, you. God gave me a dream this morning, and in it, I saw you. You were standing at a crossroads. Messengers above were calling out what I am about to tell you. It was not a road, but a vision, leading to a task. It means, Adam, God has picked you and your life as a vision. He is with you and will be all the way."

Adam fell silent over what the prophet told him. It rolled around in his head, not landing anywhere. "You'll have me up all night pondering that."

"You might as well give up because it's not for now."

Adam arose the next day refreshed. After breakfast, he rode off from the nicest town he expected to see for a long time.

CHAPTER 25

PLEASANT OR BITTER

Leaning against one of his mules, Adam held the hoof up and examined it. He carried all the necessary tools for the job. He had just entered Cherokee land. His breath clouded the air as he worked. Every once in a while, he scanned the darkening sky for signs of snow. The clouds were starting to deliver the speckles he feared.

After pulling himself back up and on the saddle, he rubbed the donkey's neck and stretched high in the stirrups to look for signs of an old gas station or strip mall. "I'm afraid it's time for us to find a place to stay, boy. The winds are picking up."

Up ahead stood an old beverage drive-thru pit stop preserved by its metal roof and matching sides. The growth of time and weeds encased it like a cocoon in time. He urged his animals forward after he hacked enough of the growth from the garage doors for them to enter.

Inside, he closed the doors as the winds threatened him, rattling the building. Adam checked out every room to be sure he was the only occupant. Trusting he wasn't intruding, he unloaded each animal's pack and proceeded to make himself comfortable for the night. The building provided shelter, but he needed to erect a tent, to condense an area for added warmth. Water was his next agenda. Bundling up, he took his bucket outside to look for some pump or stream. Five minutes later, he'd filled his bucket from a hand pump in the back of another building.

"Help! Is there anyone out there? Help!"

Stopping, Adam shaded his eyes against the biting wind as he surveyed the land to figure where the call was coming from. Faint in the wind, it called again.

"Where are you?"

"Oh, thank God. I'm over here!" The voice kept calling out.

He followed it, crawling up and over what used to be landscaping. There, he found a shivering old woman propped against a tree. She started laughing in the thrill of seeing him.

"What happened? Can I try to lift you up?" Adam stooped beside her and shouted over the wind.

"Yes, yes. I just can't get up by myself, dear. My knees are not helping me at all, and I have nothing to pull myself up with." As she spoke, Adam lifted the mere slip of a woman and steadied her.

"I took shelter in that building over there. Let me get you inside." She gave no argument as he half carried her inside. The building shielded from the wind, but as night fell and the storm increased, the space was little better than a large icebox. Adam placed her into his tent.

"I'm going out to start a fire. Here's some dried meat. Keep wrapped up till I come back."

She smiled at him. In no time, he had a fire going on the cement floor. Inside the fire, he placed bricks to heat up. Next, he started boiling water. Several times, he went back and checked in on her. He carried hot bricks in to the unexpected guest.

"Thanks." She continued to smile.

Adam went back outside, returned with a cup of hot water, and placed his choice of dried herbs in for tea. He called to her and handed her a cup. "Here's some tea. This will help."

"It won't be any good without some of this, sir." She reached for her pack and pulled out a honeycomb. When she gave it to him, he put some of it in her tea. Then she disappeared back into the tent. Adam made do for another two hours. At last, he heard from behind the tent wall. "Pleasant is my name. What's yours?"

"Adam Stands."

"Oh, that sounds… never mind. I want to thank you, Mr. Stands, for your help. I don't think I'd have lasted another hour out there. I was checking on some hives when I slipped."

"No problem. I'm glad I was able to get to you in time. Are you still shaking? I have more warm bricks ready."

She emerged from the tent. "If I stay in there any longer, I'll be baked like those bricks of yours." Dressed for the weather, she'd tied her long, once-dark hair back in a braid. Pulled tight at the sides by the braid, her rugged skin wrinkled into a smile. She looked like her name. She marched all around as if testing out her legs. "Good as new. Now, I thank you again for helping me, Mr. Stands. I live up the road about a half-mile and will be on my way. My driveway is on the left marked by a mailbox with my name—Pleasant—on it. Come over tomorrow. I will have something special for you."

"Whoa, I don't think you should go anywhere. It's still storming out there, and you went through an ordeal. It's too soon for you to go out."

"I've lived through a lot of these winters, and I am used to them."

"Was that part of your regular winter program that left you calling for help?"

"No, but I won't be tramping around in these woods from here on." She headed out the door.

"Wait!" Adam saddled up and went after her. "Come on, Pleasant. You might as well ride with me because I'm not leaving your side till you're home."

Shaking her head with an amiable smile, she grasped his hand and let him swing her behind him in the saddle. Then she directed him to her cottage, and this time, it was her inviting him inside to warm up.

He tied his horse beneath a lean-to, then followed her up a set of slanting stairs into a cozy kitchen. Surrounded by family pictures, he savored the atmosphere and steaming bowl of soup. As he thanked her before leaving, she placed carrots and apples in a bag for him and his animals. Then she made him promise to stop back in tomorrow.

The sun rose high in the morning, melting the snow faster than it came, making it a good day for traveling. He slowed his team as they headed up the lady's drive. Other horses lined up in front of her home. When he knocked, a Cherokee man, full in chest and arms, opened the door.

"Can I help you?"

"Pleasant asked me to stop over this morning, and I'm following orders."

"Come on in. How did you know Pleasant?"

"I met her last night. She had fallen in the woods. I heard her cry for help. You said the word *did*. Is she okay?"

"She passed away in her sleep last night."

"Oh no." Adam winced. "I should have stayed with her."

"No. You couldn't have done anything for her. She lived a long life of ninety-nine years, and God called her."

"Ninety-nine. I never would've guessed her to be so old." Being invited in, Adam explained what had happened the day before. They smiled at the old woman's ways.

When he discovered they'd be setting her body to rest that afternoon, Adam decided to stay and pitched in with the digging. Afterward, they went back to Pleasant's home to warm up. Food was already in the making. This family had a different tradition: telling about the person's Christian testimony.

"Let us open with thanks to God for this woman's story." They had a moment of silence. "We shall now remember Pleasant, the youngest of three children, beloved of her parents, Jay and Little Dear Stone. She grew up in this area and received Jesus as her Lord and Savior about the age of nineteen. Two years, later she married Mel Cob, and they had two sons, Jimmy and Luke. At that time, she was just like her name, pleasant and happy."

Adam smiled, picturing the woman he'd briefly met as a girl—somehow he pictured her just the same, running through those hills, laughing in delight, and stubborn about accepting help.

"They owned a cabin in Canada," the man went on, "and spent their summers there." The gentleman's gleaming black eyes seemed to darken as he spoke now. "During that time, they partied and drank for the fun of it. But as you know, Cherokee and 'firewater' don't mix. Eventually, it took everything from them, including their jobs and Pleasant's sweetness. She was a nasty drunk. All the bad things that happened to them from drinking put her in a state of bitterness, especially when Jay left her. The next crushing blow came when her oldest son died in a car accident—he also had been drinking at the time. Luke, her youngest, disappeared. Nobody ever knew what happened to him. Bitterness lived in her gut. She at least had her two daughters-in-law who lived with her."

The speaker's eyes filled with pools of tears, in love for her and her family. He looked up as if seeing her in heaven, choking on a tightening throat as he spoke of her now.

"Then, somehow, some way, Pleasant realized she had to get back to her God. She had to get away from what was changing her and back to God's grace. She shared what she was going to do with her daughters-in-law. Ruth, one daughter-in-law, loved and understood her mother-in-law so much that she wanted to know more."

When the speaker stopped, Ruth stood and walked over to a small table. On it was a Bible—Pleasant's Bible. She placed a flat hand on it and wiped across its top. Then she picked up that old Bible, hugged it to her heart, and continued the biography. "Pleasant served her God well. She became like her name again. Pleasant raised bees and supplied honey to all of you and many, many more. She was always saying, 'One's life can be like a bee. You can reach out and sting in anger, then die. Or you can receive and give out the honey of the heavenly Father, who has made you and brings His sweetness to your life."

When each finished their thoughts, they all said amen.

The next day, Adam checked his mule's packs and was about to leave when Pleasant's family rode up. They loaded his mules with her honey, bread, and other food, saying they wanted to honor her. Next, they showed Adam the best way to cross over the mountain. He thanked them and headed out.

CHAPTER 26

A BUTTON FOR YOUR THOUGHTS

When he faced the rebuilt church in the center of Beth's town, Adam found it empty. Now he'd have to find the directions to her home. As he stepped back into the twilight, he nearly stumbled into a man passing by and hurried to ask.

"Sorry, mister, but your sister and Kyle left about three weeks ago."

"Left?" His face fell with the heartbreaking news. He was so close.

"Yep. They were having the call of God again. This town is doing fine, due to their help. Pastor Kyle appointed a new pastor over the church so they could move on. Let me take you to him and see if he can give you any more information. I only know they headed"—he waved left—"that way."

At the pastor's home, a small cedar-shingled cottage, Adam met Pastor Chet. Chet informed Adam that, when Kyle's aunt had passed away years ago, they had moved into her home. A month ago, they'd started preparing to leave. "Kyle prayed and then felt led to appoint me the new pastor. I felt it, too. The two of them left about three weeks ago. They also gave out to everyone his aunt's hidden treasures."

"Hidden treasures?"

"What his aunt kept hidden in the upper part of her house—treasures. Two items she only told trusted friends about. With those precious items, she bartered for food, wood, or anything else she needed. She was a smart old cookie. Wish I'd thought of it."

"What were the two items?"

"Toilet paper and deodorant. Two things modern man can't live without."

Adam started laughing. "Oh yeah, those could be traded anywhere for anything."

"Adam, I do have one thing for you." Chet walked to a cabinet and retrieved a letter. "Beth said you might come looking for her. She wanted you to have this." He slapped the thick envelope into Adam's hand.

Adam's fingers twitched, the newsy weight begging him to open it right there. Instead, he tucked it into his shirt pocket, the paper rustling by his heart as he rose from the wingback chair. "Would you be able to suggest a place for me to spend the night?"

"Certainly." Chet strode to the door, calling the rest over his shoulder as he headed up the stairs. "I have a comfortable guest room. And my barn has plenty of room for your animals."

Adam and Pastor Chet prepared a meal from the gifts Adam had received and the pastor's supplies. "You've had no time to read your sister's letter. I am going to head to my room for the night and study. I'll see you in the morning."

Adam grabbed another cup of tea. As he removed the papers, her curvy handwriting unfolded before him, and in the flowing script, he could hear Beth's voice. At the end of the letter, she gave him directions to where they were. He folded it and placed it in his pocket, knowing his hand would reach for it many more times.

He had followed her trail for weeks. At times, when he thought he had lost them, a sign—a wheel mark or someone they had talked to—showed the way.

After slowing his horse, Adam dismounted and stooped by a hollow. Hoof prints marked the muddy depression in the trail. His lips curved to a smile as his fingers traced the now-familiar print of the shoes on the mules' hoofs, and there, prancing along the side, were the paw prints of the dog accompanying them. They'd passed this way. He swung back into his saddle, clucking his tongue to urge both animals forward. By nightfall, he came across a place they'd camped, and his heart ached even more to catch up. A day, six days later, he crouched before a campfire. Warmth radiated inside the rocks from their camp. He smiled, shading his eyes as he peered ahead. Then stilled at a soft clip-clop.

"Don't mean to scare you," a voice called out. "I'm passing through. I didn't want you to think I was following you, so I am making myself known." A rugged, cowboy-looking man about twenty years older than Adam rode up.

"The name is Sonny, and I'm heading in the same direction as you. I've been behind you the last few days. We could ride together if you like."

"Name's Adam, and right now, I am trying to catch up to my sister and her husband. By the warmth of these rocks, they are not far ahead."

Sonny gave his horse a little kick and closed the distance between them. "I wondered why I had been seeing you sniff the ground."

"You are welcome to ride along, but I will be at a steady pace."

Eyes twinkling, Sonny chortled. "The real reason I approached you is because you're a lot slower than I am and you've been holding me back."

Late that afternoon, Sonny waved ahead. "Looks like smoke from a fire."

Adam rose in his stirrups, squinted toward where Sonny was pointing across the dip of a valley, seeing the smoke crawling up the side of a mountain. "I see it." He sank back into his saddle and spurred his mare.

"Whoa, there!" Sonny raced alongside him, easing him to slow up. "If that's them up ahead, great, but if that ain't… Well, I wouldn't want to ride up and spook anyone nowadays."

"I could ride up and call out like you did."

"Go right ahead and do that. I'll set up camp here. Come on back if it's not."

Adam called out a few times to no response. The dead silence made him nervous. He studied the ground as he approached. There were the same tracks he'd been following, but still no answer. When he reached an emptied campsite—empty except for the prints and a now-cooling fire pit —tracks from horses and a wagon led off again. He rode back to Sonny and explained what he saw.

"Show me where we are on your map."

So Adam spread out the map, studied it, and pointed. "There. Why?"

"I was afraid of this. In this area, years ago, there was a state prison. Back when they had to shut them down, they took the dangerous criminals out, shot them, and then let the rest go. A lot of those hardened criminals didn't have any place to go, so they took over an area and ran it the way they felt."

Adam's chest constricted. He folded the map, slow methodical movements as he fought for calm. "Sonny, I need your help."

Beth was inside the trailer when Boy barked. Then came men's voices. She knew the drill—into her hiding place to wait till Kyle came and called her out. She waited and waited. Then men tromped inside what she called home.

Kyle spoke up, "Listen, the dog will stay inside here, till he gets used to you. He's been edgy since I lost my wife." He walked the dog to where Beth hid and commanded him to stay.

Boy's eyes tilted to where she hid and then back at Kyle. He seemed to understand. Lying down, he took his post.

Yet still, Kyle never came for her. Later, the trailer rocked into motion.

Her heart started to race. *Hopefully, they were on someone's land, and Kyle was told to move. Or maybe he doesn't feel safe now, and he decided to move. No, there are still more voices. God, please help us!*

Kyle's hands shook. They had his gun, and he had no idea of what to do. He drove the wagon on, with one mean-looking man riding next to him. But Beth would stay put. She had food, water, and a gun. *God, this couldn't be what You had us leave for?*

Adam and Sonny led their mules as they walked, following the footprints. When they rounded a pile of boulders, the tiles of his sister's trailer gleamed up ahead, a group of riders accompanying it with a horse tied to the back.

Adam slowed their pace. The wagon turned down a tree-lined drive to a columned, three-story mansion nestled in a valley, and he eased off the path, tucking the mules and horses behind some long-gone-wild pink rosebushes.

Sonny moved toward his mule. "I'll unload the packs."

"Don't do anything till I get back." Adam stuck his gun in the back of his belt. "Stay up in these woods and watch. When I come back, we can figure out the best thing to do."

Without waiting for Sonny's response, Adam sprinted ahead. Keeping to the shadows the overgrown landscaping provided, he clambered up the hill overlooking the mansion in the valley. The trailer jostled before the front porch. Kyle climbed down, looked back at his mules, and followed the men up the steps to the door.

But where was Beth?

Beth held her breath as the movement stopped. She huddled there, listing for what seemed like forever. Then the wagon jostled into motion again. When it stilled this time, it rocked with the familiar movements and clamor of the mules being removed. Next, the floor tipped to the left as someone stepped on the staircase leading in. Boy began barking and growling. The door slammed.

"I can shoot you now, dog!"

"Oh, leave him till the morning. It's too dark to shoot."

She waited again until she felt the time was right. Then she grabbed her gun and crawled out, creeping through the deep blackness. She knew her trailer, but when she eased her head to the window, it was so dark she couldn't tell where she was or which way to go. As quietly as she could, she opened a window. The smell told her where she was—inside a barn.

God, what do I do? Please, give me wisdom.

Squinting her eyes as if it would help, she also noticed she was holding her breath when Boy put his paw on her as if to say, "Come on. What do we do?"

"Facts, Beth!" she said to herself. "Think of the facts. One—Kyle never came back for me. Two—they are going to shoot my dog. Three—I must get out of here. Four—*now!*"

Moving through the trailer's darkness, she was able to find her coat and shoes. That she did fine—until she tried to leave the barn.

The horses didn't like the smell of Boy. Trying to set off an alarm, they snorted and kicked walls.

There! She was able to see light leaking around cracks from a back door.

She took off for it, only to stumble over something in the dark and stifle a yelp as her knee slammed the dirt floor. Boy licked her face as she rose to her feet. She hoped she picked the back of the barn. She groped along the wooden door for the latch, eased it up, and inched the door open a crack. Pushing herself outside, she froze. Now she listened as she let her eyes adjust and took in her new surroundings.

A fence line stretched out to the right of her, so she ran along it, skimming the terrain for a place for her and Boy to slide under—all while glancing back constantly to see if someone was coming.

Now, what should I do? Lord, I am so scared. Please help me! What would Kyle tell me to do? I can't go in and rescue him. I need to get to cover!

In the moonlight, she hiked away from the house, heading up in the trees and rocks. Boy held his nose to the ground. Then he sniffed the air and ran up to her, sitting on her feet and keeping her from going on.

Now what? She gripped the gun and aimed.

Adam hunkered behind a four-foot bush, noting every detail of the house. After an hour, someone approached in the dark. Rocks clattered under their feet as they walked as though in a mad scramble, toward him with a dog and a gun. He readied his gun, then did the only thing he could.

"Beth it's, Adam."

She jumped. Her gun went off, just missing him. Together, they faced the house. Strangely, no one came out.

"How did you find us?"

"I've been tracking you for weeks. What's going on?"

As she told him what she knew, Sonny's horse trotted up. The three hid in the dark, filling each other in and trying to think of a logical answer.

Sonny gave a deciding nod. "I'm going down to see if I can see anything."

"I'll go with you." Adam rose to his full height, tucking the gun back in his belt.

"No. One is quieter than two. Stay with your sister. If I get caught, Kyle won't recognize me, but I'll fill him in."

After Sonny left, Beth asked, "Who is this Mr. Sonny?"

"I don't know." Adam stared after the man who offered to talk into danger for him. Then he murmured, more to himself than to his sister, "I met him today."

Sonny made his way down the hill and crept to the lit windows. Weeds helped conceal him. Adam squinted into the darkness as the man's shadowy form drifted to another window.

After moving around, he lingered by one opened pane. Then he headed back to give the report. He faced Adam, his expression grim. "They never heard your gunshot because they're all drunk. But it's worse... much worse." He shook his head and eyed Beth. "I don't like what I heard—I didn't believe it at first."

Adam's sister slapped her hands on her hips and glared at him, reminding him of the determined girl she'd always been. "For heaven's sake, just say it."

"These are the type of people you've only heard about—or maybe you haven't even heard about them, ma'am. They're going to have entertainment tomorrow in town. Kyle and another man will be the entertainment."

"What kind of entertainment?" Adam rubbed his jaw.

"Trust me. You *don't* want to know. We only have until tomorrow to get him and the other guy out."

Adam closed his eyes, doing his best not to let his imagination fill in what Sonny was saying. Focus, he needed to focus. If they were going to get out of here, they'd need transportation. "Where are the mules?"

"I'll take you there."

Beth and Adam had a hard time falling asleep. Sonny, however, was asleep in peace in no time. Adam woke to Sonny packing up his horse.

"Leaving?"

"In a way. I'm heading into town, to snoop around."

"I'll be ready in—"

"Nope, you're not going."

"I can't sit around here."

"We need to stay low, and I need to gather information. Trust me, Adam?" The man was sure of himself.

"For some reason, I trust you, Sonny."

"I pray God will have given us a plan by the time I get back."

That's the first time he mentioned God.

Five hours later, he returned smiling.

Adam met him as he was dismounting. "What did you find out?"

"They have an arena once used for horse shows. That's where they gather for their sick entertainment. I've planted some helpful items that I found around there."

Beth walked up, stepping around fallen branches before bracing a hand on a nearby pine, her eyes sure and steady as she faced Sonny. "How do we get my husband back?"

Sonny gave her a quick nod before directing his response to Adam. "The way I read it, they will bring him and the other guy to the back of this place. Adam, you and I need to slip in and hide before everything starts. Then you need to wait for my cue to free Kyle."

Adam interrupted, "What will that be?"

"Don't worry—you will know it. We don't know if our guys will be tied or chained or who knows what." At those words, he turned to Beth. "Beth, you need to be outside at a waiting point with your dog, watching for them to come out. When you see them, lead them back here as fast as you can. Do not stop or come back for me. I have plans." Sonny described the inside and added notes of exits. He never told them what his plans were.

Adam and Sonny headed over to the arena. Sneaking inside, they were happy no one had arrived yet.

There, Sonny reached out and shook Adam's hand. "Take your time to make a spot." He pointed to the stalls. "Like there. See if you can see inside the arena. I'm off. We can do this!" Then, with one last nod, he melted into the darkness.

Adam scanned and scurried from one covering spot to another testing them out, seeking a place he could get in and out of undetected but with a good vantage point to keep an eye on the audience. The first stall provided the best place. He hunkered down, pushing into piles all sorts of junk. Then he checked his gun, covered himself with a tarp, and waited.

Sonny disappeared into the arena. In a half hour, the hoots and hollers from those arriving echoed through the open building.

Anytime now.

The back door was pulled aside, and horses drawing a portable cage holding Kyle and another man clomped in.

"We are going to have fun with you gentlemen tonight!" The man held a cattle prod and cackled as he poked hard at Kyle, making him scream out, then gasp. "Are you going to pray as we torture you, pastor? Or will you curse your God? We have our bets going, and I could win a lot of whiskey if you curse God. If you do, I promise your death will be quicker. If you don't, I can make it last a long time." He hopped onto a wagon and uncovered a table holding torturing instruments. Then he brandished a blood-dried knife. "Oh, sorry, I never cleaned this from the last guy. Do you mind?"

Kyle turned from him. Facing the man he was with, he ministered with words and prayer. And ignoring them, their captor placed the cage key on the table, then sauntered away, whistling.

In the center arena, a twenty-foot square platform stood. Those coming in cursed and laughed, drinking to heighten their mood. They never noticed Sonny lowering himself from the roof by a rope to the platform. But Adam did. "What on earth is he doing?" Crouching, he knew he needed to continue with his quest as he kept one eye on Sonny.

That's when some of the audience started to notice. And as they did, they drew the others' attention to Sonny. But not knowing who the newcomer was, they seemed to assume their leader, Phil, and his team did.

"Ladies and gentlemen, welcome to tonight's event."

Adam even startled and spun around at the sound of Sonny's voice.

Those in the back area stopped and huddled closer to the entrance to see the change of plans. "Who is that?"

"I don't know. Maybe Phil brought this guy in."

The place fell in a hush.

"Folks, you are going to be blown away by tonight's event."

As Sonny talked, Adam took this cue. His back hugged the dark dusty stalls, and while the guards watched Sonny, Adam made his way over to pick up the cage key on the cutting table. Hurrying back behind the cage, he reached around unlocked it.

Those watching were about to turn to the cage when Sonny shouted, "God has something for you to hear. 'Jehovah, The Maker of us all…'"

"What is this?" someone yelled.

"Who is this guy?"

A few muscle-bound men puffed themselves up as they moved toward Sonny.

"Ah, ah, ah! I wouldn't do that if I were you." Sonny held up a button. "If any of you move any closer, I'll push this. It connects to a whole load of dynamite I stole from you earlier. And where is it?"

He winked, quite a showman, seemingly enjoying his spotlight. "Right under your seats and all around this building. You gentlemen in the doorway, want to come a little closer?" When they didn't move, Sonny fingered the control. "I will not hurt anyone if things go well. You want things to go well, don't you?"

They moved in about three feet, then stopped.

"Now that's thinking correctly. I'm going to give a little talk, and you're gonna listen. It will be up to you how this will end. My name is Sonny Racker. You may remember hearing about me years ago. I was the pastor jailed for stealing millions from those who followed my ministry. I lost everything and everyone God put me in charge of. Today, I asked God for one more chance to do Him right. I don't care if I die doing it. You all are going to listen to me."

Sonny gave his best sermon ever, feeling the Spirit pulse through his veins and whisper in his words, hoping Adam and the others exited the back door to safety and reached the meeting area.

When he finished his speech, he looked into the eyes of the men and the rest of the audience. And he saw no fear of God, just unbridled anger.

"Are you sure?" He gave them one more chance.

In the dead silence, came the click of a gun, and he pushed the button.

CHAPTER 27

FE FI FOO FUMM...

Searching the homes of the group that died along with Phil was now a must. Basements to attics of each and every house, their barns and any outbuilding not left unchecked.

And in them, they uncovered eleven more men in chains. And, after how they all had been treated, the poor souls were mentally in chains. These men's physical conditions were deplorable. What they wore and their bodies hadn't been washed in who knew how long. They found the minds of these people were like beaten children. At the time of their freedom, their faces should have shown signs of happiness, but they were serious, nervous, with eyes casting down. Adam and Kyle went right away to find them all new wardrobes. Man was disappearing, but trails of his abundance still could be gathered from numerous places. After boiling a vat of water, Beth handed each one a bar of soap. They knew what to do. Still, in the end, she had to shave some of their heads.

Kyle, Beth, and Adam talked as the men rode in the back of their wagon. Beth pleaded in their defense. "We need to move on. Take them away from this horrible place. These men's minds are being held prisoners, all because of what they have had to live through here. They may not ever be able to escape the nightmares, but they sure don't need to wake up every morning and face this lousy place."

"I don't know." Kyle rubbed his chin, and his sad eyes focused on the table. "Beth, hauling twelve men around to who knows where and into who knows what may not be the best answer. I feel God wants us to set up housekeeping here, make this a place they could call home."

With no other answer reaching out, they took what they had and started the preparations of finding a home for all.

They already inspected the homes now left empty. Phil's old mansion had the most bedrooms, plus a guesthouse for the three of them. First, they had to release the animals from in and around the area before they suffered a cruel death. Kyle thought this job would be good for the men's minds, but still, there were moments they broke down and wept. It took them two days of working together to complete the job.

These men who been kept like tortured animals were so small in their spirits, causing them to be like little brittle grasshoppers. And in their minds lingered giants they had no idea how to fight.

On the third day, Beth and the men were sitting in the kitchen of their new home. She tried to work with the group, asking them a question like what they used to do for a living. When Kyle opened the kitchen door, he stepped in before Adam. "Okay, gentlemen, we're all going out for a ride. Adam and I have hitched up a wagon and want you to see something."

The men followed like sheep… except one. Walking up to Beth, he touched the counter beside her, tracing the green tiles. "I used to be a cook. I never told anyone because I swore I would never cook for any of *those* people." His head stayed bent, but his eyes looked back and forth from the floor to hers. "If you want"—the slow whisper of his voice swept through the kitchen—"I could help you?"

Adam studied his sister. Eyes shining Beth understood what this man was really saying. She reached as if to touch his arm, then drew her hand back as if afraid she'd hurt him. "You go on, Mr. Carter, and see what Kyle wants you to see, and when you come back, I would be honored for you to join me."

As the man nodded and scooted through the door, head still down, Adam met his sister's gaze, pride and love swelling his heart. Then he nodded and joined the others, leaving her to scurry away. Adam took his place in the front of the wagon while Kyle helped the rest of the men on.

As the wagon curved the overgrown brush, Kyle spoke up. "Men, as we ride around today, God wants me to make something clear. See that house over there? God says for me to tell you it now belongs to you." The wagon with its silent occupants rumbled through the broken ground, weeds tangling in its spokes until Kyle cleared his throat. "See all this land we've been riding over? All of it and more now belongs to you, gentleman. God doesn't want you to be afraid of it. He trusts you men to make it into a land of milk and honey. Everything now you see, He gives to you."

They drove on, no one saying anything. Then one fair-skinned, once-blond man cocked his head to Kyle. "Why? What good is having all that land, and what can it do for me?"

"Mr. Jordon, you may not understand now, but when God gives something to someone, it is for their enjoyment."

With the men out, Beth began a makeover on the house. She wanted it to look more comfortable and a lot less like the last hideous tenant. Beginning in the front room, she started taking everything down, tossing it into a pile. *First, the guys can haul this stuff—*

Rap. Rap-rap.

Her heart slammed her chest. Boy leaped up barking. He ran to the door and sniffed the cracks, then continued to bark. A figure behind the smoke-colored glass stood still. Beth's heart began to thump....

The men aren't back. Now, what do I do? She held on tight to Boy's collar. Opened her mouth and then shut it when no sound came. "Yes?"

"My name is Rae Ann. I know who you are, and I live in this town. Could I have a chance to speak?"

"How do I know you aren't armed?"

"Because of this."

Beth peeked out the crack of the door. The woman, Rae Ann, extended a well-used Bible, and the stiffness in Beth's shoulders loosened as she opened the door wider. "Come in. I'll be holding onto the dog."

The woman edged in. She eyed the room and Beth. Haggard features drew her face down, but high cheekbones, delicate chin, and pretty eyes suggested once, a long time ago, she had been nice-looking. Mostly graying hair framed a deeply lined face accented by pleading eyes. The woman's hands shook as she fussed over holding onto her Bible.

Still standing, Rae Ann shifted her weight, cocking a hip to brace the Bible. "I'm not sure if you will believe me, but I never was one of those others. I came here when I was thirty, and I had to exist by… well, I sold myself." Her eyes searched Beth's.

When Beth said nothing, keeping her face unchanged, Rea Ann lowered her gaze. "Anyway, two months ago, a man was killed by Phil and his team. In his things, I found this Bible, and for the first time in my life, I read it. I believe now God brought *you* here." She wiped her face from the tears flowing down her cheeks and then brushed her hand on her pants to dry it before gripping the Bible.

"The day I heard Phil was going to torture Reuben to death… I…" She struggled to speak while crying and shaking. "I prayed to God. Could He please help this poor man? Please, help us all. Yes, I knew about these men they kept for torturing entertainment. I tried but could do nothing to help them. Really."

Bringing both her hands up to her temples, she rubbed them across her temple back and forth hard and then dragged them down the sides of her face.

"The next day, I heard about your husband, the preacher being caught. So, I figured my prayers were no good.... They made things worse. But also, that same morning, I saw a stranger come to town. In desperation, I was going to ask him to take me with him, sell myself again—I didn't care. Trying to catch up to the man from a distance, I got confused when I saw him backtracking all the way back then behind the arena. He was going through a bunch of the old sheds and buildings. Then he carried dynamite into the arena. That's when I figured out what he was doing. So every time I thought someone started to go near the arena, I fooled them away. I did watch out for him—that I did."

She gave a firm nod as though to assure herself, even as she was crying so hard. Beth hugged the woman as she rocked back and forth, taking a few minutes to close her eyes and calm herself. "Each time they had one of those *entertainments* of theirs, they would come and force me along. They liked to watch me go mad from the sight." She stopped and gathered herself, but now, her eyes flashed. "But this time, I outsmarted them. I drank whiskey till I passed out. They sure must have tried to get me up, for I has a lot of mean bruises." As she held her head up high, some of those bruises glowered from her chin and neck.

Horrified, Beth laid her hand on the woman's. "May I ask—it's been a few days—why haven't you showed yourself till now?"

"When I woke the next day, it was already noon. I remembered about the day before and looked out my window. I couldn't see anyone so I ran down to the arena." She shuddered. "There it was, all blown to pieces. Birds were picking at it. Then I remembered all the locked-up men and went to look for them, but they were gone—all gone. I couldn't figure it out." Her lips trembled. She wiped her nose with her sleeve. "I thought maybe some of Phil's team might have taken them to the arena that night. The next day, when I went to scavenge for food, I saw you all and watched you till I figured it all out."

The back door opened, and the men tromped back in. Walking into the front room, the twelve sighted Rae Ann. They greeted her with hugs and tears. This woman spoke the truth, and she was what they needed—their friend.

The next few years were good to the minds of these twelve and Rae Ann. They were able to put off the old thoughts, replacing them with good ones, and that led to the toppling of their mind giants, leaving behind smiles graced with peace. But, sadly with time, also comes unavoidable alterations. A constant change varied this group's numbers from sixteen to ten to five. Until one day, only Adam and Beth were left. Adam, already eighty-nine had been Beth's caregiver for more than a year. After a series of strokes, she could no longer see, walk, or feed herself. Then came the day she also joined the Lord.

Once again, Adam took a shovel and started the job of having to dig next to where Kyle had been laid to rest. During this lonely job, no one remained for him to talk to, but God.

"God, why did You not tell me my job in life was to be a gravedigger? I stand here alone with no one to help, and I know there will be no one to do this job for me." Placing his foot on the shovel, he pushed down again. "Oh, Father, I don't mind doing this for my sister, but I am pretty old and depressed thinking of the number of graves these two hands have dug."

Tears were slipping from his eyes, heating his face as they followed the craggy wrinkles before dropping onto his hands. Freeing one hand to hold onto a hanky to tend to these tears, he dug.

After several hours, he patted the last bit of the dirt and sat before he could walk away. He watched a cricket on its travels. Something still alive.

CHAPTER 28

RIGHT OR WRONG

It only took three weeks for the stillness to torment him. Complaining to God one night resulted in a dream—a dream one knew was from God. In this dream, he stood in a watch store, enjoying its many fine timepieces. The store owner handed him one finely crafted watch, and when he turned it on its back, he saw his name inscribed there. Next, the dream jumped to a group of people who were patting him on the back, saying, "Oh, we see *now* you can help us, for you have the *time*."

In the morning, Adam rose out of bed and went to a full-size mirror. There, he examined himself, for he could pass for a much younger man. Not only had he retained his strength, but if he never looked into a mirror, he could forget his age entirely.

It was time to pack.

Throwing a leg up over the saddle, Adam then settled down and rode to the end of the driveway, stopped, and turned his mule around. He looked back to what was his *last* home for many years. Now, as he stared at it, doubt crept into his mind. He could envision each room and the comfort that came with it. Then, remembering the echoes of loneliness in each of his steps, he turned his mule and pulled the other to follow.

Soon Adam grew accustomed to traveling again, including learning how to maneuver around the many overgrown plants. Those vines could still take a toll on him. If unattended, plants could show who ruled the earth. It was as if they knew they had been there first and were working to take back what was once theirs. Small trees now towered with stretched limbs stopping the undergrowth beneath them. And under them, Adam found it much easier to travel. Even the empty houses were being broken apart by hardy plants, giving the appearance of the houses being folded down and the plants reclaiming their dead.

"You were right, Pa." For he had been warned of this. "And I needed this map to understand the lay of the land." He always studied the map with precise accuracy. Especially now, with where he was heading.

Here and there, Adam came across visible bones of someone who had passed on. Years ago, he would have taken time to bury them, say a little prayer, but now, he had to speak to God about all this. "Why pray now, God? My prayer can't change anything for any one of them. And now, I find I am too old to continue burying my fellow man. So, if You don't mind, from now on, I will just tip my hat in respect of Your creation?"

With no argument from God, he did just that.

The traveling went well for months. One night when his supper was ready, he poured himself some herb tea and studied the map. Yes, sir, he was heading in the right direction. Rusty signs of confirmation poked their heads out here and there.

"You know, Father, I haven't seen anyone at all during these months, and I don't understand it. Many people used to live way past my age." He paused, sighed, and spoke what was on his mind. "Maybe I was all wrong… about the dream. Is all this traveling my will or Thy will being done?" He whistled a bit as he thought. "Either way, I'm almost there, and I'm wondering what it looks like after all this time. Not that I was ever there, but tomorrow could be the day I'll find out. Oh, and maybe, since I am heading north, well, maybe they all were heading south."

The next day, after his morning constitution, Adam came across a mother duck on her nest. *Ah, breakfast.* As he stooped over the nest, the mother's warning was not only noisy but also threatening. He might have to kill her. He'd killed his food most of his life. He raised one arm to take a strike, when an Old Testament Scripture verse popped into his mind. It was about leaving a mother bird to live if taking her eggs or young. The result, it said, would be it would be well with one and that one may prolong their days.

How strange was that old law, Father? I guess it was teaching about how to take care of our food chain.

He took his bruises, pushed her away, and removed only what he needed in an act of kindness and obedience because there was no way *he* could deplete the world's supply of ducks.

Four more days passed before he found himself on the outskirts of this once great city. At this point, his mules were stumbling. He dismounted to inspect the problem. Crouching, he brushed grass from an obstructing mound, then stilled and rose. He was passing rows of overgrown graves. The graves of those who had fought for this country. Carefully gauging the lines of the rows, he passed without disrespect or obstruction. Ahead, if nothing had changed, a wide river snaked against this city—so how would he cross?

The walk as he got closer was quite nice. He and the mules crossed a beautifully flowered field. Beyond the city, the sun attached itself to the sides of its tall buildings. The whole thing reminded him of Dorothy approaching Oz.

This was the country's capital, Washington, DC. Here laws were birthed, aborted, or remolded into what man thought they should be. Yet this was all funny to him because, no matter how hard man tried, his *millions* of added laws could never become more powerful than God's Ten Commandments.

As he came to a bridge, Adam's old job from the road department came in handy again. Inspecting his end, he found this bridge to have been well-taken care of, probably because of the importance of the city connected. Still, he walked his mules across instead of riding, inspecting each and every step. Reaching the other side, he paused to envision what this place might have looked like in its day. But years of being empty, with never-ending abandoned cars, buses, poles with wires, gave this city a science-fiction jungle look. He first toured Lincoln Memorial and then Washington Monument, but their decaying left him disappointed.

He and the mules traversed what was left of the streets. Because safety was always his number-one concern, he'd soon have to find a place for him and his mules. Hoping he had enough time, he followed signs toward the Smithsonian Castle. And just in time because rats—very large rats—slunk to the streets. Scurrying from one shadow to another, they studied him as they ran by. Shuddering, not wanting to camp out with such hungry vermin, he pulled his mules up the front steps to the great doors of this vast castle.

There, it hosted a sign: "Please come in, but close the doors after you!"

At first, he felt it wrong to bring mules inside, but the lack of any humans and the abundance of rats changed his mind. And he loved being there. After setting up for the night, he had a meal of dried meat, fruit, and his famous herb tea. He found a map in a desk that not only gave him a tour of the building but also of the city. The place had been stripped of valuable items, but history still loomed everywhere. The next day he toured every inch of it—all that was open to the public eyes and the parts never viewed but by privileged eyes.

Feeling like he was on a vacation, Adam headed over to one of the buildings he came to see, the Capitol Building. As he approached, eyes focused on it, he forgot to seek signs of someone, or some ones, still being around. He rode his mules up the many steps and planned to spend the night or nights. Two days later, he moved from that building to another and another of interest, leaving the White House for last. And the whole time he never sought the signs.

One day later, Adam ambled up the lane to the White House with more curiosity than any of the other buildings. But the closer he drew, the stranger it looked.

Where those—yes, *cows* grazed in the front. Goats trimmed grass edges, and chickens roosted all over. Then peacocks screamed an announcement of his arrival.

A man stepped out of the front door. Hands tucked in his pockets, he sauntered with an action of no concern. "You took your time getting here. I hope you enjoyed your tour."

How did he know?

"You can tie your animals over there. It's a good grazing area. Then come on in. I'll have something for you to eat. Oh, and welcome to the White House." He disappeared inside.

And soon, Adam edged through the door. "My name is Adam Stands, and I thank you for the invite."

"My pleasure, Mr. Stands." The man led the way to a room with food prepared where he invited Adam to sit. "Let me introduce myself. My name is George—George Washington. Yes, yes, that's really my name. I came to work here seventy long years ago, and I haven't been paid for sixty of them."

Adam grinned. "Well, if you think I've come to settle your bill, Mr. Washington, you have another guess coming."

They smiled a gotcha look.

"How did you know I have been here touring the city?"

"I spotted you on the bridge when I was up in—well, if I tell you, I'd have to kill you."

"Keep it to yourself, then."

"This is an odd time in life to take a tour, Mr. Stands. What brings you here, or would you have to kill me if you tell?"

Adam explained who he was and why he was there. George told stories of his youth, being on a team that was more or less the janitors. "Now, I run for president every four years to which I hold an official election. You not planning to run against me in the next election, are you?"

"You are doing such a fine job, I see no reason."

They chatted for about an hour before they needed to tend the animals. George gave him a tour of the grounds, even pointing out his gardens. "I keep some of the animals locked up in the East Room at night. You've seen the pack of rats about, and they aren't the only things. But if you don't mind steps, which I've seen you don't, I have kept the Lincoln bedroom for guests. And it's my gift to you, so you don't have to pay."

Adam didn't want all those stairs to climb, but who could pass up such a chance?

The next morning, he couldn't stop praising the bed. "Now, I know why you stay here. It's the bed! I have never slept on anything so comfortable in my life."

That day, he was given a tour of all tours of the White House. The stories George shared were never dull. But when asked what happen to the last President, George looked away, gazing at the photo of the last President. In the lengthy silence, a sheen glazed his eyes. Finally, he faced Adam. "He hung himself."

Again, he looked away, his shoulders sloping. "Maybe it was the stress of it all. He was elected the same year God took back His gift, and you know the history. Those years, no one was taking the time to run for President, or for the real matter, no one even wanted the job."

He shook his head and wagged a finger. "After that, the people who served him up and left. Me? I waited till they were all gone. Then I had the place to myself."

"Don't you miss people?"

"Oh, at times. But this place was home, and it had all I wanted or needed."

Adam spent the next weeks being granted to see places he never knew about and listening to George's never-ending enjoyable stories. Two weeks later, he prepared to leave. George couldn't get Adam to stay, and Adam couldn't get George to come. "Besides," George winked, "if someone else comes through, they might be able to cover my back pay." He had handed Adam two huge sacks tied together. "Throw these on your mule. They could get you through some tough times."

"Thanks. What is it?"

"Government rations."

"Any good?"

"They will be if you are hungry enough."

Adam turned his horse but stopped and called out. "Mr. President?"

George paused, turned, and smiled. "What is it, Mr. Stands?"

"Make up a ballot for me for the next voting and please make a mark next to your name for me."

"Can't do that." Waving his hand, he turned, then called out, "If you're dead, it won't count. And the law is the law."

Before Adam passed by the United States Supreme Court, he studied Moses' sculpture holding the Ten Commandments. Staring at it, he couldn't help thinking about the reasons for a President, for Judges, the Congress, the Senate, and all those thousands who worked here, once upon a time. "God, if I see it correctly, if it weren't for sin, they would have all been out of a job."

CHAPTER 29

THE COUNT DOWN AND UP

Exploring empty towns always interested Adam. There he gleaned from the leftovers of other men for his survival. Folks sometimes left notes of instructions such as where one could find matches or ammo. Once during his searching, he enjoyed a man's fully stocked woodworking room. There, he created a comfortable backrest for his saddle.

Too bad, I hadn't thought of this contraption years ago.

He complimented himself every time he hooked it on or took it off. Adding to his comfort, the previous owner had a lightweight folding chair including a table to replace his old ones.

As he approached the southern states, he came upon a few older folks. The more he headed south, the more numbers grew. One thing he enjoyed about those he met was the fact they had pretty good personalities. They were also independent, and most of them had a strong relationship with God. Each time, he would stay to visit, satisfying everyone's need for human contact. But after a few days to a week, he always felt he needed to move on.

One day, looking up, Adam saw a sign confirming his location as he inspected his map. There, instead of being hidden behind brush, was its population sign, standing tall and visible. Initially, its numbers were slightly more than 50,000. But then there were extra signs with extra markings. They bore the marks from being crossed out time and time again, showing numerous counts of the years as it dwindled. At last, there was a small, neatly hand-painted sign proclaiming the number forty-seven, with a date of only a month earlier.

If that's true, that will be the most people I've seen in one place for years.

Rising in his stirrups, he scanned ahead for anyone belonging to those enormous numbers.

Yet his first reception was of wood smoke and bacon, making Adam oblivious to everything else. A wider path led to these attractive odors. He hoped whoever was cooking was as inviting as the smells.

Adam's mule snorted, and as the sound went out, he saw a figure at the road's edge, standing and staring in his direction. From it came a woman's voice calling out, "Aaron, we have company!"

Somewhere around the bend, came a faint man's voice. "Who is it? If it's Levi, tell him I could use his help."

"It's a stranger with two mules."

"A… ranger?"

"Not a ranger… a *stranger*."

"Oh, we have company."

Adam smiled his best smile, tipping his hat. "Good morning, ma'am."

"And a good morning to you, too, sir." Youthful-looking for her age, she stood tall, seemingly in good condition. One hand held a bucket of berries and the other a staff. Putting down the bucket, she held her hand over her eyes, studying him in the morning sun.

"Your name doesn't happen to be Adam Stands, does it?"

In unbelief hearing his name, he could hardly answer her.

"It does. Do I know you?" He squinted back, studying her face.

"I've never met you before. But when I was in prayer this morning, a name came to my mind, and I couldn't shake it. Go figure how God works." She picked the bucket of berries up. "You must be a pretty important man, Mr. Stands, for God to announce your arrival."

When Aaron walked up, she introduced them. She added about knowing Adam's name.

Adam dismounted and shook Aaron's hand. Then he turned to the woman. "I'm of no importance, Miss…?"

"The name is Lula Bell, and don't argue with God. He gave me your name, and here you are. Are you a preacher or something?"

"Not at all. But I am a Christian and have been all my life."

"You're kinda scrawny. Have you eaten?"

"Nothing that smells as good as the bacon I keep whiffing." With one finger, Adam scratched inside the cusp of his ear.

"Then come up to the house after your done helping Aaron with whatever he needs help with, and I'll have something ready for you to eat."

"Yes, ma'am."

Adam followed this man, Aaron, to where he was trying to fix a fence. The man wiped his nose with a hanky and then gestured for Adam to hold part of the fencing.

"Mr. Stands, you must realize God speaks to my wife differently. I used to complain to God about it. In fact, everyone did. Didn't think it was fair of God. Then, one day, we learned the hard way that God didn't take to our disapproval. He showed us in His Good Book that He can talk to whoever He wants about whatever way He wants."

As Adam tried to comprehend what he just said, Aaron added, "And if you know what's good for you, try not to complain about it with Him. It can rile Him up something awful, ya know."

"I must admit, I've never had God speak to me. You could have knocked me over when she said my name."

Down the path, the woman walked away, toting her berry pail in one hand and her staff in the other.

"I wonder why God revealed my name to her."

"Don't know. But I sure appreciated God sending you to give me a hand." Aaron looked up to the heavens and said, "Thank You."

With his two extra hands, they fixed the fence swiftly and securely—much to Adam's relief because his stomach couldn't stop begging for that home cooking. When he followed Aaron with his mules, the path led right up to the back of their home. From where he stood, more back doors of small, modular homes faced him. Lula Bell stood at the door, watching as he came up. "Come right in, Mr. Stands, and you can wash up." She headed toward the kitchen.

"Please call me Adam."

"Nope, it's Mr. Stands till I feel otherwise."

Aaron smiled and threw up his hands, showing that he conceded years ago. "She can be stubborn."

They heard her click her tongue. "I heard that, Aaron."

A knock at the door interrupted them, and Lula Bell strode into the front room. Adam heard her answer it.

"Yes, there is a stranger here. And guess what. God gave me his name this morning before he showed up." A pause followed as someone else spoke. "Because I was able to ask him if it was his name before he had the chance to say it." A pause again, "Give the man time to eat, and then we'll all meet in the card room." She closed the door and returned to the kitchen. Standing in its doorway, she looked at Adam. "What is God up to, Mr. Stands?"

Adam, still thinking about the food, pulled a chair out from the table without an invitation to sit. His stomach had been living on very little of late. "The way I see it, Miss Lula Bell, since He talks to you, why not ask Him?" He picked up a fork, hoping they'd take the hint.

"Good idea. Please serve Mr. Stands, Aaron, and I'll go talk to the Father."

Adam hadn't left a crumb after his second serving and was helping with the dishes when Lula Bell came back.

Aaron gave her a peck of a kiss. "Well, what did the Man have to say, dear?"

"Not a thing. He can be stubborn."

Adam swore he heard God say, "I heard that!"

On the way over to the card room, Aaron shared how they purposely put all the homes in a circle so they could keep an eye on one another. From there, the land fanned out, used for everything from gardens to animal stock.

"I used to travel a lot before I met Lula Bell," he said. "During that time, I met a woman who had her gardens built up. Figured they would be easier for her to tend later in life. Thought it was a pretty good idea, so we did it here."

Then they went inside, greeting the people called Little Israel. For one hour, they asked questions, and Adam shared about himself.

"You are right, Mr. Stands. There seems to be nothing special about you." One man folded his arms, lips twisted.

They talked for a while longer, sharing about their lives before he noticed some had fallen asleep and others were heading home for a nap. Adam stood, needing to stretch his legs. Then some of the men patted him on the back. "Well, at least one thing we do see about you is you have been given time like the rest of us."

Adam's spirit quickened, remembering his dream from a year ago, but he kept this to himself.

The rest of the day, they spent opening a small home for him and tending his mules. Not only did the women and men help clean and air out this new home, but they also gave him delicious food for his lunch and supper.

That evening, Aaron stood at the door to leave. "One more thing. Tomorrow is the Sabbath, and we all meet in the synagogue at ten a.m. Oh, the card room also doubles as the synagogue."

"Synagogue?"

"It may seem odd, but we no longer call it church," Aaron said with a flick of his hand. "Since the Good Book says we are the church, we try to respect each other that way, and a synagogue is a place to worship and learn. But it's not law—call it what you want."

"I'm looking forward to it. Good night and thank you and Lula Bell very much for everything."

"Lula Bell says to come over for breakfast till you get your supplies, about eight a.m.?"

"Sure," Adam said, yawning.

When Adam joined the others seated in the synagogue, Aaron took a head count. These, he apparently did daily to be sure all was well. But only forty-six was the count, one short. After the count, he added Adam's name. Then the worship songs commenced.

After a few moments of their singing, Adam couldn't help but close his eyes and take in the magnificent sounds of their voices blending as they sang one of his favorites. They weren't just singing, but worshiping. Accompanying them was a sweet mix of two violins. Here and there, Adam studied Little Israel.

Earlobes, noses, and chins had grown longer with age, and wrinkles varied. Gray was the only color of everyone's hair, if they had any. And beards hung long on most men, giving an Amish look. Yet this group was different from the others he encountered. They had spirit—not just spunk —and a spiritual oneness connected them.

This morning worship lifted Adam's spirit. He never knew it was down. But being able to worship like this again was like times long ago.

After the service, Adam walked over to a window while he waited for Lula Bell and Aaron. A white dove fluttered down and perched on an empty limb. It squeaked little calls at him. With a screen on the window, it couldn't be talking to its reflection. He whistled back, assuming it could hear him. Tiring of it after a few moments, he moved to the next window to see its view.

As he looked out that one, a great light filled the window like an unexpected flashbulb. He jumped back. The same dove hovered where the flash was. Its wings spread out, and its belly faced him. For a few seconds, it stayed in that position, not falling, nor flapping its wings. It was so beautiful, and then it was gone.

He looked behind him to see if anyone else had seen what he had. But the small group left was busy, and they weren't included in this vision, except Lula Bell—she was at an angle watching him. Turning back to the window, he stared. How could one explain what he saw? He thought about it all day with no real answer.

Adam rose early to feed his mules. An unfamiliar man in overalls walked up. He didn't remember meeting him in the last two days.

"Good morning, Mr. Stands."

"Please, the name is Adam." Adam wiped his hands on the side of his pants and then grasped the remarkably strong hand being offered to him. "I must apologize. I have met so many people here.... I seem to have forgotten meeting you."

"Well, that's because we haven't met. See, I don't attend the synagogue. My name is Levi, and I've come to welcome you." He turned to face the mules. "I'm pleased to see you know mules. They are mighty fine animals, aren't they?"

"These two have been serving me well for more than thirty years. I've been keeping my eye out for some younger ones, but I haven't come across any—maybe never will."

"You may have to change what you just said if you come over to my place. In my barn, there happen to be two new little ones, no older than two days."

This he had to see. Levi's eyes twinkled, and Adam felt he'd made a dear friend. Walking to the barn, he saw Lula Bell with her staff facing them in the distance. He waved.

The young mules interacted with their mothers, and each had its own distinct markings. "So, what are the names?"

"I haven't named them yet. But, seeing as I've named a lot of animals in my life, how about you take a turn?"

Adam leaned on the gate and studied the two until he came up with what he felt led. "Well, that one is the smallest, but wise in how he handles himself. And the larger one seems somewhat stronger, but as I watch him, I can see he's careless. So how about naming little one Jacob and Esau for the other?"

"That's from the Bible?"

"Yep, you don't mind, do you? It seemed to fit."

"No… no, no, no, that's fine." And the man sighed. Adam found Levi to be quiet from then on.

For the next few days, all went well, their friendship developing, till he mentioned one of the little mule's names. Then something like a wince twitched through Levi.

Each morning, the men teamed up working on the pen for Adam's mules. Holding up an old two-by-four, Levi spoke up. "I'll be changing colts' names."

"For some reason, that doesn't surprise me. I figured it has something to do with you not attending church." Adam stopped sawing a board to face Levi. "I'm sorry, Levi, for putting you through some sort of pain."

Levi started to excuse himself but changed it to a confession. "Adam, my life was not so nice. I have done a lot of bad things in my time—really bad things. So, I'll let you know right now I am not at all worthy to be a Christian." He pointed behind him. "And don't think that group of nice folks back there haven't explained how God forgives and forgets. But I am not worthy and will not reach for something I don't deserve. Can we just leave it like that?"

"Sure. But I'm not changing my name—how about you?"

Levi's head dipped while he thought. Then he lifted it and smiled at Adam. "Ah, you got me on that one. Perhaps I was taking it a little too far."

Lula Bell walked up with a container. "Thought you two could use these." She lifted the lid, revealing four biscuits inside. Along the side, she'd nestled gleaming jars of fresh-cooked quince berry jam and milk. "You are lucky I happen to love to cook *and* God told me to bring you this."

Grinning, Adam relieved the gift from her. "Well, thank Him for us, Miss Lula Bell, and I thank you for being the willing servant."

"Thank Him yourself when you say your prayer before you eat. You wouldn't want to get sick or choke on it. You don't mind waiting, Levi, while Adam says his prayer?"

"No, no, not at all."

"And you're welcome from me. See you men when you bring my dish back." She took her staff and headed toward the house.

Levi pointed to the wagon. "Let us take a break and enjoy these biscuits while they are warm and the milk's cold."

Adam bowed his head and quietly gave thanks, then settled back and layered a biscuit thick with jam, eating it in quiet bliss.

Levi took a spoon of jam and lifted it to the light. "Years ago, my older sister told me when I was around five I had mistaken a jack-in-a-pulpit seed for something edible. Apparently, my throat swelled so bad I could hardly breathe and almost died."

"That must have to have been horrible."

"I don't remember it at all. She said I was struggling for every breath. She said it was quite traumatic. But I have no memory of it at all." And he shrugged and spread the jam.

"Not at all?"

"Nope, nothing."

"Well, friend, that's how God is with your ugly ol' sin." Adam took his last bite, licked his fingers, drank up his milk, and stood. "When Jesus shed His blood, God's memory of your sin vanished. He just can't remember it."

Levi's breaths quickened. His eyes locked on Adam. "Not at all?"

"Nope. None. Not at all."

Levi just sat. He pulled and played with his beard. "Adam, I think I get it."

"Don't matter if you get it; it only matters what you do about it." Adam winked. He walked back to where he was working, and after a moment, he glanced up to see Lula Bell with her staff on the knoll. Just above her head, a dove fluttered. Then, with grace, it flew above Levi.

Levi was praying.

CHAPTER 30

WHERE IS ONE'S HEART DURING A SACRIFICE?

Looking down at his belt notches, Adam was happy to see his short time in Little Israel had to put weight back on. That started him thinking of breakfast, which started his feet to head to his guesthouse kitchen. This group of people had a nice agreement about cooking. Instead of trying to cook for one or two, they gathered every few days and discussed the dinner meals. They decided what they could be and who was to cook what. One might bake bread; one might make a roast; another desert.

By now, it had been a couple of weeks since Adam had arrived, and he was trying to decide about moving on or staying. Goodbyes were nothing for him when the itch came. But the itch to move on *this* time was quiet. Maybe it wasn't even an itch at all.

He asked God that morning. "What should I do? Move on or stay?"

"Who are you talking to, Adam? Do I need to ask old Doc Pete to come over and take a look at you?" Lula Bell stood by the screen door, holding a basket—which usually meant it had something pretty good in it.

"Good morning, Lula Bell. When one is by himself... oh, never mind. What brings you here this early in the morning?" He held the door open for her, took her basket, and eased it on the table.

"Two things. One, here is some of my friendship cake. The yeast starter I used for this goes all the way back to my grandmother. Amazing, isn't it?"

"I have seen people always use the same yeast starter. I never knew it could go back so far."

"And it was given to my grandmother by an old friend of hers. So, who knows how far back, maybe all the way to Adam and Eve themselves."

Pushing back some stray, fallen hair, she combed them with her fingers. "Next, in a few days, it will be the start of Rosh Hashanah. We celebrate it here by nine days of checking our relationships with one another. Then, on the last day, we have a revival."

"A revival?" He broke into a laugh.

"Don't you laugh! You think it's silly, Mr. Stands?"

"Oh, pardon me, Lula Bell, but I find it… well, rather odd. Because of our ages that would be even needed, if that's the right word. This is a fine group of people, with a great love for God."

"We are sinners, Mr. Stands, plain and simple. And *especially* at our ages, we could use all the reviving we can get. Come if you want, it's not law. But it is good for you."

"I wouldn't miss it."

"In fact"—she pulled a drawer open, then picked out a wooden spoon and waved it in the air as part of her words—"why don't you take a turn by preaching it? It doesn't have to be long, just fervent."

"Me?"

"Yes, you. Why not you? Yes"—she gave an emphatic nod—"that's a great idea, Adam. Thanks for taking a turn, dear." And out the door, she went.

He just stood there, replaying what happened, trying to figure how she had just gotten her way. *She's good.*

Later, Adam sat with a Bible at his kitchen table to study up on Rosh Hashanah. *Hmm… it says here there are ten days of making amends with one another, and then it ends with the Day of Atonement. The Day of Atonement is a finishing up with God, one-on-one. Kind of like the Lord's*

Prayer of "Forgive us of our trespasses as we forgive those who trespass against us."

And last, there are three parts. First, one was to suffer, second, a priest was to go to the Father on your behalf, and last, a scapegoat. But all that was already done by Jesus.

Adam closed the Bible and rubbed the back of his neck, twisting it this way and that to ease the kinks. To his right, he'd left a cupboard door open. He pushed back his chair and rose to close it, then paused. Was that…? Yes! Another door hid inside it.

He lifted mismatched dishes and dented pots out of the way, grasped the nail serving as a latch, and opened this hidden door.

Inside, bundles with notes attached to them formed a small stack. Three, to be exact. He read the notes several times over, eager to discover some sort of treasure the previous owner had saved. But the first treasure caught his eye. Studying it, he got his sermon.

Lula Bell stopped to visit several times during the next few days, snooping to find out what Adam's plans were. She even threw out some direct questions like, "Have you been studying?" or "How's it coming?"

But Adam would smile and say, "It should be fine." And leave it at that.

In the nine days leading up to his taking a turn, this snug group was reminded at the daily count to recheck their hearts and be sure all was well with one another.

Afterward, many of them would come up to Adam, telling him how much they looked forward to his preaching. To which, he would only remark, "God doesn't pick those equipped. He'll have to equip whomever He picks."

On the day of the revival, Adam kept busy all morning, preparing for his turn. Yet, after lunch, he found time to slip in a nap. A rap on the screen door woke him. Aaron stood there, waiting to be invited in.

"Come on in, friend."

"Thank you." Aaron tried to head right into the kitchen, but Adam slid in front of him.

"So, Adam, I was wondering if the yeast starter I took off Lula Bell's batch worked out for you." Aaron was not only giving a hint, but his eyes were looking in the direction of the kitchen.

"Oh, it worked out better than I thought, thank you very much."

And the two fell silent for a moment.

"Walking by, I couldn't help but smell that you had been baking. Was that with the starter?"

"Why, yes, it was."

Silence again, and it was driving an invisible wedge.

Aaron finally gave up with a grumble, bidding Adam a goodbye, claiming he had to get back to work.

Adam readied his other ingenious idea and pulled it up to the synagogue. He not only had it covered, but he'd tied it shut so tight that no one could just peek in. Then he went back and toted over other supplies.

Just before the meeting, he placed the sermon on a garden wagon and pulled it up and into the building. The wagon was given the place next to where he was to preach.

When everyone arrived, they seated themselves and studied this curious wagon. The songs seemed a little shorter than normal that day, and while the people sang, their eyes strayed a cloth draped over a container on his curious wagon.

Lula Bell stood. "As you all know, Adam Stands will be preaching tonight. I am not sure what he has in mind or under that cloth, but I, myself, am ready to hear him lead our revival."

As Adam stood, taking his place, applause thundered through the gathering.

"Thank you." He cleared his voice. "I was taken aback being invited to speak on this day, yet honored. And I must admit I had to study up on these Holy Days. But as I did, I learned it was a time the people were expected to make amends with each other.

"When that was done, one could go to the heavenly Father for forgiveness. Like the Lord's Prayer, 'Forgive us our sins, as we forgive those who sin against us.'

"And it was also to be a time of great sacrifice. Very important sacrifices in order to receive the Lord's forgiveness.

"I saw all of you do the one"—he lifted his voice, his gaze moving tenderly over his new friends—"but not the other. So, today, I have supplied the sacrifice."

Mumbles flowed through the group.

Adam walked over to the wagon, gripped the curious cloth, and pulled it off. A box. Next, he asked two of the men closest to him to help lift the box from what it was covering. And there, under the sunlit window, rested a cake—a large cake, glistening with a creamy white frosting.

Delighted gasps whispered through the group, one woman clasping her hands together while another clapped. "Oh my!"

Adam grinned, sweeping a hand toward his concoction. "You are looking at a genuine, old-fashioned red velvet cake."

"I can barely remember what something like that tastes like, and yet my mouth is watering!"

"Oh, *I* remember." Beaming, Mr. Turms, the shortest man, rubbed his hands together. A tear slipped from his shining eyes. "Mom used to make it for my birthday. Never thought I'd *see* one again, let alone get to taste it!"

Adam pointed toward Lula Bell. "Now, we have to thank Lula Bell for her yeast starter. Because of it, I was able to make the required cream cheese frosting."

"A cream cheese frosting!" Delighted whispers swept through as they turned to one another.

Adam proceeded then to cut a large slice, revealing the white cake's rich red interior.

By this time, from their expressions, no one was thinking revival, but rather, *Will I get a piece?*

"Please, follow me outside."

They shuffled outside, following this tasty delight from years ago.

Adam worked for the next few moments pulling at a tarp to unveil his *next* masterpiece. A large rectangular fire pit, about four feet tall, constructed from scrap metal. Next to it was a pile of wood, stacked as though ready to be lit. Now the eyebrows lifted, and a few furrowed.

"Sacrifices are funny things," he continued. "Unless there is pain, in one way or another, they aren't worth anything."

"He's not going to burn that cake, is he?"

"No, he's not! Is he?"

"The man's insane."

"Lula Bell, do something."

As the different type of murmuring echoed around him, Adam acted as though he didn't hear any of them.

"Aaron, Levi. Could you please help me lift this cake up and into this pit? Come on now. I know it's one delicious red velvet cake with cream cheese frosting, but there must be a sacrifice."

The men leaned back and shook their heads.

"Guys," Adam chided, "today, I am the preacher. Do as you're told."

The men looked at each other, then gave up on Adam's reasoning. Together, the three placed the cake inside the pit.

"Stand back, please," Adam blustered. "I don't need any of you to be a sacrifice also." He walked around the container, adjusted the insides, here and there, and then picked up a dirty rough log, and to everyone's shock, tossed it inside. They gasped in horror!

Lula Bell rushed forward and grasped his forearm. "Adam, now you're being cruel. You didn't need to ruin that beautiful cake. No matter how perfect the cake was, it couldn't top what Jesus did on the Cross."

"Exactly!" he said. "But I thought…"

"This was to be a revival." She softened her touch and her voice, a crackle vibrating through it. "We were to be revived in our spirits, not, well, upset about a beautiful cake."

Adam picked up another log and threw it in also. Then straightened and scanned those gathered, reading their expressions, their disbelief and no longer lingering hope. *No!*

"Oh, I see." He circled around the back and picked up the last log. "A revival should be like celebrating one's birth in Christ? Yes, yes, I see what you mean." He picked up and lit a candle and dropped it in with some kindling.

One lady pressed her hand to her mouth. Lula Bell buried her face against her husband's shoulder. Mr. Turms fisted his hands.

Adam went around to the front, then faced the firepit. Unhooking a low front door, he pulled out a long drawer. And there, proud as can be, sat the coveted cake. Untouched.

"Why, you old scoundrel!" The lady lowered her hands from her mouth, laughter flowing out.

"Oh!" Lula Bell lifted her face. "You about broke my heart over that cake, Mr. Adam Stands."

Mr. Turms slapped his hands against his thighs. "Now, that's a revival!"

Adam and the men carried the cake back in. He served all the people nice large slices.

When they were content, he shared how he had found the hidden recipe with the stashed ingredients, including the meaning behind the trick.

The rest of the day Little Israel couldn't stop talking about it. Not only did they love the lesson in the treasure, but claimed it the most fun they'd had in a long time.

CHAPTER 31

AND WE WEPT WITH OUR COMPLAINTS

A month later, the morning count came up short. Joseph was missing. A volunteer group headed out with Lula Bell in tow. Then returned with news: their dear friend had gone on. Many started to cry, others were solemn, and reality was back.

Joseph, the graveyard caretaker for twenty-five years kept it trimmed and ready. By this time, each person's grave had already been marked so they knew their future resting spot. And because of that, no one liked to visit the place.

During the years, the newer graves' depths had to go from six feet deep to barely three because of the ages of the men who dug them. And with the shallower grave depths, problems arose, like critters scavenging or the unwanted smell. This thought plagued the men who did this harsh impending job.

But for now, they needed to wrap Joseph's body in sheets and roll it in a sling. Next, they took his empty shell by cart to his marked grave, and nineteen men dug.

The day he died, and he was buried. It had become so ritual it was like one taking out the trash, and no one felt comfortable about that at all.

At the next morning count, Aaron spoke up for Lula Bell.

"Gentlemen, we need to come up with some idea about digging the rest of our graves. We should have dealt with this problem years ago. But, selfishly, we left it to poor Joseph."

After an hour of discussion, they concluded that all the able men were to start digging the needed graves. Get it out of the way. After the next morning count, they would start.

The nineteen men set out to do the digging. For the first hour of the first day, they disturbed the soil, and then they stopped. It was a tough job —rough on the hands, feet, backs, and more. Nevertheless, they needed to continue until they completed the job. Figuring at this rate it should take them about forty days, they expected it to go smoothly. But things took a turn.

"It just ain't right, digging one's own grave!"

"I have a shoulder that could go out at any time, ya know."

"Well, if I'm dead, I don't care what you do with my body."

"That's fine for you. You'd be dead. But what about us, who'll have to tend with your old stinking, decaying body?" As more of them in agreement inserted more opinions.

"How did Joseph do it? I have to stop now and quit." And with that, Eric Meribah stomped to the shade.

It had only been fifteen minutes, on the third day, and many followed him away.

Each morning, more excuses and fewer workers showed.

Meanwhile, Adam had picked a place for himself. Aaron and Lula Bell worked on their promised land. But, seeing what was going on, Lula Bell needed Aaron to speak up about this problem.

"Dear friends of Little Israel, this job—a job we all agreed upon—is not getting done. And we need to address this. I know this is a very physical job. But God is here with us, and He will help us if we stop complaining."

Eric shook his shaggy head, bushy brows narrowing and creeping into one. "Why is God making this so hard on us? This time of year, it's unbearably hot, even working in the morning. I feel like I will die. Is that what He wants?"

The others grumbled their agreement. So, Lula Bell said she'd take it to the Lord in prayer.

In the morning, when they reached the graveyard, an enormous cloud had settled over. And every morning from there on, it was built up again. But after a week, the people grew accustomed to it and started to grumble again.

"Oh, Aaron, this ground is so hard and dried out." Eric poked it with his spade. "I have worked on the same spot for three days now, and it's only the size of a tire, a small tire at that. Is God making this so hard that we just drop dead on top of our own graves? Because at this rate, that's what will happen."

So, Lula Bell took it to the Lord again.

And in the night, it rained. It rained and softened the ground, and the people rejoiced. It did so every night. But seven days can take a miracle and make it into nothing more than a daily occurrence.

Lips pinching tight and jaw jutting, Eric Meribah spoke up for the men. "This is it, Aaron! There is no good way for us. Yes, He has given us a cloud and rain. But now, the ground is heavy from the water, and the weeds are overtaking us. We will die, and there will be no graves."

The man sat, and others proceeded to weep.

Lula Bell slammed her hands on her hips, eyes flashing. Blisters seeped, staining her dress in little spots when she moved them, and she stood stooped over, not straightening to her full height as was her custom. Adam ached seeing how this job had taken a toll upon her. "You want to complain?" she demanded. "You want to grumble and act like those who caused this world to cease? Well, I'm done!"

She stomped up to Mr. Meribah. "You, sir, may have my grave, for I have decided I will not go into that Promised Land with any of you." And she left.

Adam found her, hours later, sitting by a stream soaking her palms. She offered him a rueful smile.

"Listen, Lula Bell, this may not be my place to say anything, but if I don't, I feel I would fail you as my Christian sister and what our Father in Heaven has taught us… to talk things out."

Before the night could pass over her house, she knew what she needed to do. She first apologized to Adam, and next in the morning, she would to the others for her temper. She was in the wrong for her lack of love and patience.

When Lula Bell arrived at the morning meeting, she was relieved to see none of them were missing so she could address them all.

"I'm so sorry, folks. I'm thankful for this chance to ask you for your forgiveness. Yesterday, I acted unloving and unkind. I apologize."

Lula Bell's friends held no grudges. Even Eric gave a wave of his hand and mumbled his apology. But did he do it out of a polite response and still hold a grudge? She needed to ask, away from the others, to be sure.

Aaron was napping after lunch. *Ah,* she dried her hands on a cloth, *a good time to clear the air with Eric.* And she headed to his home. But there was pinned a Gone Fishing note to his door, so she knew right where to find him.

Working her way down the path toward the river, she enjoyed gleaning a few blackberries along the way. Soft trickling sounds of water teased her ears as she rounded the last curve of the path. There he was at the water's edge, Mr. Meribah. He sat fishing, his socks and shoes tucked beside him, his feet dangling over the surface, his shadow cast toward an old boat beside him.

Eric looked up when he was aware of someone. "Welcome."

"Eric, about my apology yesterday… I would never want to hurt your feelings, and I need to be sure you knew that."

"No problem, Lula Bell. I can stir up a lot of strife in my old age, and I also need to be reminded to face God with more respect and trust. I promise the men and I will start back up later today, and we'll all finish the job."

"Thank you." She plunked onto a bow of the old boat to rest. Then, after a few minutes, she climbed in it to sit more comfortably and bask in the sun.

After a while, Eric puttered to his feet. Gathering his string of fish he said she should come along.

"Yes, Eric, I should," she conceded. "But I seem to need some help getting up and out of this boat." She planted her staff and tried to pull herself up with it. "I must have sat here too long." Before he could put down his fish, she grabbed her heart and fell back to the floor of the boat.

"Lula Bell!" he called.

Aaron and Adam were deep in a chess game when Eric found them.

"Lula Bell!" He was so out of breath. "River! Boat! … Heart!"

The men rose and hurried to get to her. But as they rounded the last bend, a stronger current that had been rocking the boat, caused it to slip into the water and drift away. The river current, strong from the last rain, then pushed the boat out from the growth of cattails, preventing them to follow.

They could never catch the boat, and Lula Bell drifted away.

CHAPTER 32

I WILL MAKE YOU MOVE

Adam remained with Little Israel. The people now needed each other more than ever, physically and mentally. One by one, they were crossing over to their Promised Land, dwindling their amount after many years to three—Adam, Aaron, and Levi.

"I thought women were to outlast the men?" Levi said one night at dinner.

"Oh, I think this is best this way." Aaron poked at his food. "After all, like those mules of yours, this life would be too hard for the women to handle. Nope, God knows what He's doing."

"Adam, you're the youngest and in better shape than the two of us put together. Could you remember when I go, to put me in Lula Bell's grave?"

Shoving his plate away, Adam scowled at the table. "You have told me that for *five* years. If you don't quit, I may put you there before you're ready to be put in." He leaned forward and gave Aaron one of those looks.

Aaron sighed. "I guess I'm coming to the age where I'm starting to repeat myself."

"Starting?" Adam raised an eyebrow.

"Yes, *starting*." Aaron shook his head like a kid trying to make a point.

Levi stood to take his plate to the kitchen. "I never noticed."

"That is because you're so forgetful." Adam folded his arms across his chest and bent back, raising his chair to its hind legs. "And you don't remember any of it."

"Any of what?" Levi asked.

"Never mind." Adam gave up and went to bed.

He tried to sleep that night, but some animal growling in the distance awakened him, causing him to toss and turn, worrying about their stock and themselves.

In the morning, at breakfast, he mentioned it to the men.

"I might have heard some animals, but with my *bad memory*"—Aaron lowered his head and eyed Adam—"I have forgotten."

"Sure, you remember that from last night. But let me ask you this: Why did you just put your plate on the floor?"

"For the dog!"

"We don't have a dog!" Adam scooped the plate from the floor.

"I had a dog." Levi forked a mouthful of eggs, then repeated his favorite story about some old dog named Cooper.

Heart heavy, Adam excused himself from the tale he'd heard a dozen or so times and left to do the morning chores. *It sure would be nice to have a dog. A dog could protect the stock and us from whatever was out there growling last night.* But there hadn't been any pet dogs for years. So he dropped the thought and checked the pens while keeping a loaded gun within reach.

Finding everything tight and none of the animals missing, he still felt reluctant to let the penned animals out to graze.

That afternoon while he was dozing, a sound woke him. He sat up, eyes sleep blurry as a couple of small animals in the house walked right up to him. Two puppies?

He must be dreaming. With no fear of Adam, they stopped in front of him, cocked their heads, and gave a what's-up look.

Aaron must have left the front door open.... But any dogs around now were wild. *Where's the mother? She's not going to be happy about these pups.*

He grabbed his gun and stood on the porch scanning the area. The pups followed.

He placed them on the ground below, figuring the momma would be back soon. He waited and watched. Meanwhile, he sized up the pups to be about six weeks. One had short smooth copper fur, looking like a hound, and the other was black with white places, but softer and longer fur. Both bellies were full as they tumbled around playing with each other.

But how did they get up those steps? When he stood on the porch, they whined to get up and couldn't do it themselves.

No mother showed up that afternoon. Aaron and Levi came in after fishing. Aaron flashed a grin. "I told you we had a dog!"

Adam fed the pups milk and scraps and invited them to sleep in his room for the night in an old crate. The mother never showed.

Around midnight, Adam woke hearing one of the pups growling. Figuring a potty break was due, he carried both out and placed them down to seek a spot. But the little one growled again—toward the chicken coup. Adam grabbed his gun by the back door and approached in the moonlight.

There, busy digging, a big old coon got ready to raid. *Ka-boom!* If not done, the coon would have returned till it accomplished its goal. Back in the house, Adam studied the copper pup, wondering how that little one knew and how they had gotten in the house.

In the morning, he reported what had happened last night, for neither man woke to the gunshot. Levi looked down at the copper pup, "Just like David in the Bible, huh? You're so tiny. But you still went after the big guy. So, who is your brother?" From that day, they were known as David and Jonathan. And a team they were.

Adam enjoyed teaching the dogs to guard and hunt. And in the next two years, they became his best friends as Adam lost his other two.

Adam was doing all right for a while, till one day gruesome body parts maybe from his old friends were scattered around his yard. They had been dug up and dragged around by wild animals. One was a skull.

He headed over to the old graveyard site. And there were diggings—lots of digging, with body parts strewn around.

He couldn't do it. His mind couldn't face cleaning up all he saw. Adam almost crawled back to the house, shaking and lamenting all the way. The only response his mind formed was to move on—quickly.

CHAPTER 33

THERE STOOD A MAN

Since, his exodus seven years ago, Adam found his traveling even harder. When the weather was good, his old body could only make about five to six miles a day. Then he would again face the task of setting up a new camp for the night or longer. Jacob, his mule, was more than thirty years old now, and Adam himself was too old to do the work as before. Sometimes a task took so long he fell asleep doing it. Sometimes, he fell asleep after he and Jacob started off. Who knows how far he traveled, or if he traveled at all.

This time, he pledged to keep Jacob's gear loose, should God take him. Then his dear friend could escape the harness and wagon.

"Hey, David, old buddy, would you and Jonathan help him, huh? Let's go now. It's so nice outside, and I feel good."

David lifted his nose to the air.

"What is it, David?" Adam reached for his gun and listened, then decided to continue. But he kept more alert.

As he walked toward an opening in the woods, he stopped Jacob. He smelled smoke.

"Maybe we should turn around?" He released his grip on the gun and withdrew his map. "This shows a river to the southeast."

His gut tightened, for he couldn't move quickly anymore. "Jacob, what do you think? These fires can move awfully fast." But as he studied the dogs, they showed no fear.

Then—could it be? His heart leaped. Yes! Those *were* footprints in the well-worn path—a path smooth and straight, unlike the more familiar animal-trail path. And in the hard laden mud were shoe prints.

People!

"Friends, maybe God has changed His mind."

Thinking this could be just as surprising to others, he started calling out as he followed the path. "Hello! Is anybody there? Hello? Hello." Dogs barked in the distance. Then came farm sounds—sounds that put life into his ears as beautiful as the finest symphony ever played.

Chickens and goats squawked and brayed, being stirred by the dogs. His heart beat hard. Almost running to the sound, he followed what looked to him as a clouded stone in the distance. But now, getting closer, it became clearer. A home with smoke curling from its chimney, and standing in front of the barn was the figure of a man.

By now, he could only shuffle up to another very old man. He had never moved or called out. They just stood and stared.

I must be so scary to look at. I am dirty, with a wild mess of a beard and hair. He is clean and combed.

Finally, he offered his hand. "I am Adam, and I haven't seen anyone for over seven years. Are there more of you?"

The old man, who was slow to speak, shook his head. "Nope." Then he spoke again. "I am Noah."

They searched each other's eyes. Then Adam shifted his weight to another leg. "I had a friend once named Noah. When I was little, we played that I was the Adam in the Holy Word, and he was the biblical Noah."

"I, too," said the old man, "played with a friend named Adam, when I was little, that same game." He narrowed his eyes, squinted as he cleared his throat. "Adam Stands was his name."

His aged voice quavering, Adam said, "Noah, it is me—Adam." A grin caught up his words. "After all this time, Noah, God brings you to me."

"No," Noah spoke with almost a command. "He brought you to me." He smiled. "Come now and let's tend your animals. Then we can go inside to talk and eat. I am too old to stand here without sitting."

As he spoke, Adam remembered his momma's old saying: Many hands make light work. And they did.

Noah wobbled to his wood stove as Adam looked around the warm room.

"Sit now. I have chicken soup here. Since it is the Sabbath, it has already been made," Noah said as if he had planned to have company all along. "I'm sure we have a lot to catch up on."

"How do you know it is the Sabbath?" Adam gawked at Noah.

"Well, let's see, I have been keeping count since my wife passed away and because God the Father requested it. Who am I to argue with Him?" Pointing toward Heaven, he shook his finger. "He is the one in charge. He was the one who led me to gather all my animals to live with. He taught me how to start again with nothing when the people were gone. He is all I have, and I trust Him."

Adam felt nervous inside. Maybe he was upset from all that just happened. But, as Noah gave thanks for this meal and their friendship, a peace fell on him. They talked into the night with the strength of young men.

Noah and his family had become Messianic Jews when they moved on. He and his family listened to a rabbi who was preaching on the street one day. The man taught that there was never to be two testaments, as the old and the new, but only one—the whole Bible, God's word. But his family continued asking questions about his Jewish Jesus, and when the teacher answered all of them, it became clear this Jesus was the Messiah.

Noah later became a rabbi. He spoke of his wife and how they survived all the changing years. Adam shared the basics of his life, but he had no wife.

"Well, with God, nothing is impossible!" Noah winked.

Adam stopped and looked at him. Then they both started laughing.

That night, when they could talk no more, Noah made Adam a bed, and Adam felt as if he were home again.

"It's time to get up, Adam. Your sleep interrupts my wanting to hear your voice again."

Adam awoke, still feeling peace that morning, as if it had not been so many years without hearing another person's voice.

Why was that?

In the morning as soon as Adam had gotten up, Noah fed him breakfast. Next, they proceeded to fix him a well-needed bath. Noah cut his hair and even trimmed his face. As Adam fingered his clean hair, he started to remember the days and nights of loneliness. He shuddered and had to look into his friend's face to snap back into the present. Adam rose and stood in front of Noah's full-length mirror, shocked by seeing this old man and wondering how awful he must have looked before the cleanup job.

"I ask you, Noah, who was that old wrinkled-up man I saw in your mirror?" He chuckled. "I think, by the looks of it, you have now started a home for old folks." He patted Noah on the back. "But I thank you, dear friend, with so much of my heart than I can never put into words."

Adam pointed his finger toward the door, shaking it in determination. "You have chores to be done. So let me help. We can do them together."

Noah led him outside and explained all about his farm of goats and chickens. He could not provide for cows, but he had a small donkey for pulling. "These animals must live off the land," Noah said. "I can't do the work for grain and hay anymore."

Adam straightened as best he could, drawing in a full breath as he surveyed the marvelous things Noah accomplished. *Life here is good.*

CHAPTER 34

NOT TOO OLD TO LEARN

For the next two months, every day was not only peaceful but also filled with the two old men's stories resulting in laughter and tears. They daily joined in Bible reading and prayers. Adam found he was still learning many things about the Bible from his friend the rabbi.

He flipped through his Bible's thin pages. They still rustled past his tender touch. "Why is it I am a hundred and twenty-five years old and still discovering this old Bible as if it is never-ending?"

"Well, I learned something from an old preacher years ago. The man was explaining God's written word. He said the Bible is shallow enough that the youngest babe shall not drown, yet deep enough that the wisest man shall never touch the bottom."

Adam thought about it, and even though there'd never been any children in his time, he felt the answer was right.

One morning after the chores and a good meal, the men sat and rocked in their favorite chairs. Noah leaned forward and looked Adam in the eye.

"Adam, I have been teaching you so much about the Jewish ways... I feel I am preparing you for some great task that God wants you to do."

"My dear friend, I have heard that on and off my whole life. Look at me. I am old. You're old. What would God want me to do now, in this very old body?" He held out his cracked and gnarled hands. "These hands can barely feed me, and these old legs of mine, they couldn't walk a straight mile if they wanted to."

Holding up both his hands like he was stopping traffic, he added, "He could have used me when I was young and when there were people? Do you see any?" He tightened his creaky jaw and rubbed his tired eyes. "Maybe I already did this thing I was to do. Besides, with my name and your name and the time of our birth, it brings that type of thinking on." He sighed, settling more comfortably into his chair. "God is just letting mankind come to a stop because of what man has become, sin-loving and not wanting to change."

Noah did not reply. Adam found his friend fast asleep. So, after he thought of all that was said, he also closed his eyes and slept, too.

"Adam! Adam! Wake up. I had a dream. God was talking to me, and He wants me to share this with you."

Adam opened his watery eyes to Noah pointing a crooked finger at him. He licked his dry lips, seeking moisture to move his tongue. "Yes, Noah, what did you dream?"

"No, it was more than a dream." Noah shook his head, disagreeing with himself. "Maybe it was a vision. But it was clear, as clear as I am speaking to you." He coughed to clear a buildup in his throat. "I see it so clear now.... I understand."

"What is it you understand?"

"You! You, I understand." With shortness of breath and a cough, he tried to continue. "You are to shamar the Garden!" He smiled and stared down to the left. Then he bent forward again in his chair, bracing his elbows on his knees and folding his hands together, still smiling and with some sort of clarity only he was experiencing.

He gave an emphatic nod. "Think! Shamar. Shamar is a Jewish word meaning guard. It is in the Bible." He chortled, clearing his throat again.

"While in the Garden, Adam was given the job by God the Father to keep, or shamar, the Garden. But he didn't do it. We always concentrated on the sin of eating the forbidden fruit, but Adam was also to tend it and keep it. And it is he who failed!"

"So, you're saying he was to *guard* it? From what? Where does this say it in the Bible? Wait, let me think." Adam paused, thinking. He could envision the scene in his head, God telling Adam to guard the Garden. Nodding in agreement, he asked, "Now what does it have to do with me? Noah?"

He looked over to his old friend who had fallen back to sleep.

After a time of thinking, Adam now had more questions. "Noah, I would like to know." He looked over to his friend to see if he was paying attention. After calling his name louder a few times, he got up to check him. Then he knew. Noah was not asleep. He had gone to be with the One he had just talked to.

"Noah? Noah! Please! Don't leave me, Noah. Please! Please!" Adam cried and hugged his old friend. Even though he had seen a lot of death, this frightened him more than ever because now he felt more alone than ever.

After an hour, he tucked his old friend in bed and gathered all his belongings along with a few things he thought that Noah wouldn't mind. Then Adam headed back out the door to travel again but with anger and fear inside him and tears that wouldn't stop flowing. Adam walked out to find the death that still eluded him.

CHAPTER 35

I COME TO THE GARDEN

Three months from Noah's death had passed Adam was back traveling with his two dogs and one mule. His arms and legs now could no longer lift him to get onto Jacob, which was good because the last time he tried to get off, he crumpled to the ground in tremendous pain.

So Jacob was used only as a pack mule and a true friend. He was still able to carry a load of provisions, and his art of a conversationalist was to be a good listener.

Food and needed water every day were also never far. God now completely took care of him. These miracles were obvious to Adam, that his beloved God and Savior, was the one taking care of him. Serving Adam as only a father would.

Even though Noah's death was hard on him, their teaching time together renewed his spirit with the Father far beyond what it had been before.

Yet he was confused. What Noah was talking about before his death made no sense. Many times, Adam excused it because Noah was close to death, so anything could have been going on.

In Adam's daily traveling, he added singing to his praising God. Strangely, he could recall all sorts of songs from his youth. But he also made up words as they flowed from his heart to God's ears.

One morning, Adam found the weather perfect for an old man to walk in, with the sun's warm rays reaching down into his tired bones adding to his good feeling.

He folded his ancient map and headed toward the next town. As he came to the edge of this barren, hardly recognizable town, a lovely old stone church stood—intact—close to the path. Eyeing its construction from the straight spire to the stone steps and foundation, he found it looked safe, so he asked God, "Father, do You mind if we stop in and take a look inside? It still looks sturdy."

Checking around the old building, he took Jacob to one side and tied him to some brush. Back in the front, he pushed open the wood door, warped with age, and edged in. Stained-glass windows layered with dust gave a beautiful soft shine of light inviting him in.

Next, he shuffled up to the rows of pews while holding onto them. Oh how they looked like they were at attention, just waiting for people to return! A square wooden table in the front continued its job of displaying a stack of old red hymnals. Their careful placing invited anyone who entered to use them. He hobbled over, accepting the age-old invitation, and reached for a songbook. Then, with care, he paged through it.

Finding it to his liking, he decided he could sit and sing some of these songs to his Lord and God. Turning to the front pew, he didn't bother to push aside the built-up dust, but sat.

"Here, Father, I remember this one." Holding the page open with gnarled hands, he lifted his old voice, bringing life to the beautiful tune.

He sang several songs, but as he was singing the last one, "I Come to the Garden Alone," he heard a woman's old voice join in. He did not stop or jump. He relaxed and continued to sing till the song ended.

"Well, it's nice to see that you love Him, too." A sternness not presented in her singing edged the words.

He turned and found her standing in the open door. Then she spoke again.

"I thought I'd never see another human being in my life. My name is Selah. Selah Evelyn Macintosh. I come from a sturdy family of Scots, and we can be stubborn. So that's probably why I'm not dead. How about you? Why aren't you dead?" She reminded him delightfully of Katharine Hepburn in *The African Queen.*

He struggled to stand and gave a tilt of a bow. "I am Adam Stands, Adam Malachi Stands. I'm not Scottish. And to address the question of why I'm not dead? Well, I have been wondering the same thing."

"I guess we are both in the dark on that subject." A smile gentled her face, lifting aged cheeks to twinkling eyes. "I live a short walk from here. Come on home with me, Mr. Stands, and I will fix you something good to eat."

"Thank you. That will be much appreciated." Following her, he was still smiling.

As they were walking, she swept a hand to the hills. "I heard dogs barking over there. It sounded like they were hunting."

"Oh, those would be my dogs, David and Jonathan. They're hunting for their food and for mine." He pulled on Jacob for the animal tried to head in another direction. "As soon as they are done, they'll find me. They're good old boys, and my friends for ten years now."

"You don't think they'll kill any of my chickens, do you?"

"No, ma'am. They can smell the difference, and I have seen them respect them a number of times." Watching her as she hobbled down the path using two canes, he wondered what kind of woman could live this long without needing others for help or going insane.

As they rounded a knoll, the trees gave way, and he observed a large stone cottage nestled close to the woods. Vast gardens of flowers in their motley colors lined patches throughout the front and back. Vegetables overflowed the garden boundaries, and two hothouses leaned against each other on the south side. Overgrown fruit trees lined the east and west. A small patch of grass, which she must somehow be cutting, carpeted the yard. Chickens scraped and pecked the ground near a sturdy but weathered barn. Cats perched on the fences and slipped through the shadows. Goats meandered in the sun, their tinkling bells adding a melody to accompany the robins and crows.

A vast amount of different sizes and shapes of cats ran up to Selah, calling to her, bouncing, then turning curious eyes to Adam. But instead of running away, they slinked by his feet, welcoming him as if he was the master come home from a long journey. Laughing, he balanced his weight with his cane. If not for it, he would have tripped over the bunch of them.

She gave him a grand tour of the outside as they cared for Jacob. And he was in awe of what this woman was able to accomplish.

Selah explained that she and her best friend had this place made for their old age. They had sinks and counters crafted so they wouldn't have to bend over or reach too high. Door handles were levers. Everything was rethought on how they might need it from hand pumps, to railings, to raised flower and vegetable beds—so much was accounted for.

"My friend, she thought of the clever solar heating, the small hothouses, and medical supplies. She was so smart."

She showed him the inside one of her hothouses stocked with plastic boxes containing things like large print books, games, and crafts. It was all well planned.

As they headed toward the house, his dogs barked, bounding up a path. He turned to them, clutching the top of his cane while waiting to be sure what he said about them earlier would be the truth. Wagging their tails, they took their place with him. Their bellies were full and bloated. But this time, he did not have to ask them where the kill was. After they greeted Selah, the dogs settled on her porch for a good nap in the sunshine as if it were their reward.

"Tell me about you, Adam. I have gone on and on about this place, and I need to hear about you. But first, come in inside." She pointed to a comfortable-looking chair. "Take a seat there, Mr. Stands, I shall fix you some lunch, and it can be your turn to talk."

Adam told her as much of an outline of his life as he could, and that woman was full of questions. When the afternoon meal turned into the evening meal, he asked her what was on his mind, how did *she* bear it all?

She looked down and clasped her small hands in her lap, twisting and clenching the fingers. Then she said, "There were many times I didn't know if I could, especially when my best friend, Lynna, died.

"Lynna and I were one hundred and three years old when it happened, and I had to bury her by myself. No, no, I didn't have to dig her grave. We had them dug years before. But I did have to get her in it...." She closed her eyes, face contorting as if she were undergoing the ordeal again. When she gave up remembering, she said, "But I'm sure you have faced the same type of days at some time, Adam." She was so wise. "It was God who was did all the work and saw me through day after day. As soon as I give up, He gives me something else to live for."

She went over to a gray cat that slipped in. It arched its neck into her hand and started purring.

"Like the time I took to my bed and wished to just die. He had Cornelia, this gray cat of mine, have kittens right on top of me. The things were so pitifully cute. The next thing I knew, I was up tending to them, enjoying little ones running all over the place."

She reached across the small table and placed both her hands on top of his. "You and I can team up, Adam, if that's all right. If you wish to stay, you can have my friend's old room."

Adam had broken into tears.

Pushing herself up from the table, she went to his side and placed her arms around his shoulders and her head on top of his. Head to head, they wept.

The next morning at breakfast, Adam said, "Tell me, Selah, what did you think when you heard me singing in that old church?"

She laughed. " 'Oh, good! A man to help with the chores!' " Eyes sobering, she paused. "No, Adam. First, I thought God was calling me home. Then I thought my mind was playing tricks on me. But as I stood in that doorway for some time looking at you, well, it was the most beautiful sight I'd ever seen."

She didn't need to ask him the question. She seemed to know the answer.

"Also this morning, Adam, when I woke up, I smiled so much when I thought about you. And I couldn't stop thanking God, either!"

He chuckled out loud and admitted he did the same. But he wouldn't share that he wanted to go to her room first thing and check on her to be sure she hadn't gone on.

Every day, Selah made him laugh. Her humor connected to his as if they were one. They were both open and honest with each other. He broke down and shared parts of his life he thought she could bear. Including his best friend, Noah.

She shared her life stories and tales of her best friend, Lynna.

"Neither Lynna nor I married. So we had made a pact when we were about fifty to pull together and make plans for our old age, to make the best of it. It was like working on a challenging, fun puzzle. But who would have thought it would have gone on this long?" Eyes narrowing, she swept a hand through the air, gesturing to the land around them. "Or I would have made better plans."

Then Selah sat at the table and put her elbows on it, clasping her hands together and resting her chin on top. After a moment of silence, her voice quivered. "We had to shoot a man once." Her voice dipped to a mere whisper. "He had gone mad and was trying to get in our home. He yelled and screamed and waved a big knife. He said he was going to kill us for hurting him." She tilted her head and put her chin in one hand as she recalled the incident.

"We buried him and asked for God's forgiveness. We felt so sorry for that man. He couldn't help the way he was." She stopped, then jutted her chin. "But we couldn't let him hurt us."

CHAPTER 36

IT'S TIME

But the Lord called to the man, "Where are you?"

Genesis 3:9 NIV

God continued to look after these precious two. They read the Holy Word daily, and then they enjoyed prayer as one. They had come to where they didn't need to ask for anything. They didn't have to pray for someone's salvation. No bills had to be paid. No one was sick, and they didn't clog up their prayers with man's worldly needs. But most of all, they were no longer lonely.

Adam and Selah were always thanking the heavenly Father. Telling Him how much they loved Him. And strangely, as they walked daily with God, the gardens seemed to produce more blooms and fruits. God was at their helm, and they were enjoying the ride.

Then one day, while Selah and Adam were going over a hand-drawn calendar Selah had been making for a great number of years, Adam blurted out, "Well, I'll be, tomorrow is my birthday."

"Let me see that thing." Selah studied it until her lips widened into a full smile. "Adam, this is so funny how God works. It's my birthday too."

Adam itched the inner of his ear for a second as he thought.

"Since it has come to our attention that tomorrow is both of our birthdays, how about we have a little picnic at that table by the creek?" she asked. "After all, it's not every day one gets to turn a hundred and twenty-six."

One of her cats leaped onto her lap, demanding to be petted.

"Sure, Selah, that sounds nice. We can also bring the deck of cards and some play hands. But today, I will go to the store and buy you something special." He chuckled.

"Well, it had better be something expensive. I expect nothing less from my new beau."

"Oh, so now I'm your new beau, am I?" Lifting his eyebrows in a teasing way, he then rose out of his chair and hobbled over to her and searched for her in her eyes, "We are, aren't we?" Taking her hands in his, he stated, "I wish the heavenly Father would have let us be together a long time ago, Selah."

As he turned to hobble off to his room, in just above a whisper, she added, "So do I, Adam Stands. So do I."

The next morning, the sun rose hot. One couldn't ask for a nicer day for a birthday picnic. Flowers bloomed, birds chirped, the yard was alive with beauty and life.

Except Adam, when he awoke, he felt strange. He was weak, stiff, and short of breath. Alarm struck him so hard with that all-knowing feeling of what was going on inside him. His body was dying. One cannot explain the feeling that comes when you start to feel your body shutting down, but Adam knew.

He suddenly became filled with fear. Fear, like everything was going out of control, gripped him because now he wanted to live. Because of Selah, and he knew it. Then a thought jolted him.

Oh no, I can't die in her home. He struggled, rocking his body. *Get up!* He had to get out of this room. His arms shook as he pushed into the bed, finding the strength as he begged wrinkled old hands to lift him. His legs wobbled. He fought, but finally standing, he held onto the bedpost for support. After reaching for his cane, he faced the door and the challenge of taking steps—seven of them. A task had never looked so hard. Cane gripped in trembling fingers, he braved the crossing from his room, through the hall to hers. There, Selah sat in her favorite chair. Her skin tone washed to dull white and gray, and her clothes rumpled as though she'd been there all night.

She raised red, sagging eyes to him. "I'm sorry, Adam. I cannot make it to our picnic today." As she spoke, she was drooping down lower in her chair. "I'm afraid I'm dying."

"I am too dying, Selah." His throat closed, the words choking him.

She lifted her head and studied his face. Knowing crossed hers in a wince. Yes, he was shutting down. Even she could see it.

"I want to go outside to die, Adam. I want to be out in my garden when it happens."

A smile quirked his lips. Even at the end, she knew what she wanted.

"Sure, Selah. Do you think you can make it to the bench?"

She smiled at him in gratitude. "I can if we go together." Her determination to get outside gave her the strength to rise. They shuffled left and shuffled right, bent over with steps so small they scarcely seemed to be going anywhere at all.

When they reached just outside, she leaned against him. "I can't make it there."

He pointed her toward the raised garden next to them, and somehow, they both sat on it. After resting for a moment, he felt place her hand over his and, with one very old finger, brush a bit of dirt off the top of his hand. Then he turned his hand and held her small one in his.

"It's nice to meet you folks."

They looked up, searching for the owner of the voice. Out from under the brush slithered a serpent.

"I came by to say goodbye. You are, after all, the last of mankind." He spoke respectfully. "You do know you are the last?"

The serpent cocked his head as if they hadn't noticed. "Didn't He tell you? Oh, He probably didn't." He sighed. "There is no one else left on earth. The world will soon be done with mankind." He delivered the speech so sadly and then paused, tongue licking as he seemed to reflect.

"Yes, God got rid of the rest a while back and has left you two to finish the job." Again, his tongue licked forth. "He could never seem to do right by man. Oh, not that He didn't try! He even flooded the earth once and tried to start it all over again, but He never could get things quite right." The serpent swayed his head back and forth as if he were pacing.

"It was plain to see all mankind suffered because He wasn't up to the job. Sorry to say." A sad shake of his head accompanied his apologizing tone.

"Did you know there are a lot of us—gods—out there, not just one? In fact, I'm here to make you an offer because I think everyone deserves a second chance, don't you? I would like to try to fix all this." He squinted reptilian eyes as if sizing the place up to buy it.

"See, I can give you the greatest gift ever." Sudden animation quickened his slithering words. "Would you like to be young again? Not only could you be young, but you could also bear children and start up this whole world as it should have been. You would worship me. And we…"

As the snake spoke, Adam could see Selah's eyes staring off, wondering if she could see what he was saying. She was tired. She was weak.

Then it dawned on him. He understood what he was to do. It was not the literal garden he was to guard, but man's relationship with God the Father.

Feeling around in the dirt, he found what he needed. His hand wrapped around a rock. He lifted it into position. Then, under his weakened breath, he said, "I will **shamar**!"

The End

ABOUT THE AUTHOR

Candyce L. Nichols always had a creative bent in her life. Today, she's an owner of a specialty candy store in Ohio and an active writer. During her twenties, Candy mastered being an artist. Then, in her thirties, she entered the field of car sales and became a successful businesswoman. She has been part of the National Search and Rescue Association, which uses trained dogs for search and rescue and human remains' detection. Her vast experiences have led to her being featured on radio talk shows, speaking at service programs, and acting as a demonstrator of products and services for commercials and advertisements.

A native Midwesterner, Candy was born in Cleveland. She accepted Christ as her Savior at twenty-one and has continued to follow her faith. Starting with her early membership at Lake Erie Church of God, Candy has worked as a teacher for youngsters and adults.

Candy has advanced her writing skills by attending such conferences as Write To Publish in Wheaton and the Christian Writers Guilds, where she was taught and mentored by such best-selling authors as Jerry B. Jenkins, Dr. Dennis Hensley, DiAnn Mills, and James Scot Bell. Her series of Allegorical Speculative novels includes *God Whispered, The Book of Selah,* and *The Book of Noah.*

Made in the USA
Monee, IL
07 May 2023

32990031R00125